P9-CMT-874

3 5674

Chase Branch Library
17731 W. Seven Mile Rd.
Detroit, MI 48235

NOV · 2016

CH

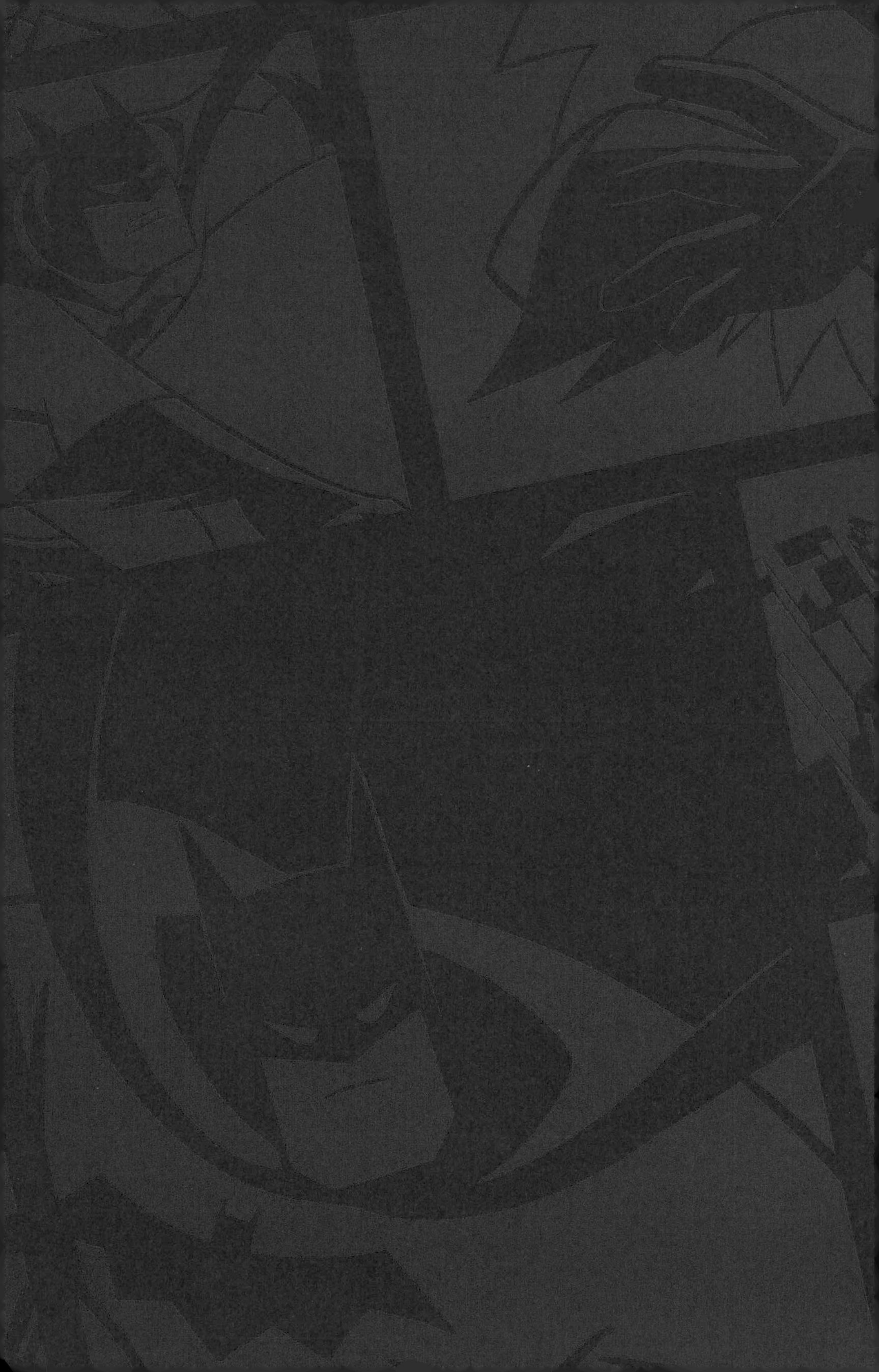

COMIC CHAPTER BOOKS

DC COMICS SUPER HEROES

BATMAN

STONE ARCH BOOKS
a capstone imprint

Batman Comic Chapter Books are published by
Stone Arch Books,
A Capstone imprint
1710 Roe Crest Drive
North Mankato, Minnesota 56003
www.capstoneyoungreaders.com

Copyright © 2014 DC Comics.
BATMAN and all characters and elements
are trademarks of and © DC Comics.
(S14)

Star33545

All rights reserved. No part of this publication may be
reproduced in whole or in part, or stored in a retrieval
system, or transmitted in any form or by any means,
electronic, mechanical, photocopying, recording, or
otherwise, without written permission of the publisher.

Library of Congress Cataloging-in-Publication Data is
available on the Library of Congress website.

ISBN: 978-1-4342-9132-5 (library binding)

ISBN: 978-1-4342-9136-3 (paperback

ISBN: 978-1-4965-0098-4 (eBook)

Summary: The Penguin asks Catwoman to kidnap the
Ventriloquist's prized puppet, Scarface. That way,
the Penguin can hold it hostage so the Ventriloquist's
gang will stop stealing the Penguin's profits. Catwoman
flawlessly pulls off the caper only to discover that the
Ventriloquist has decided to wage war on the Penguin's
forces in retaliation—and neither ultra-violent villain is
willing to back down! Not wanting blood on her hands,
Catwoman decides to team up with Batman to set
things right.

Printed in the United States of America in Stevens Point, Wisconsin.
092014 008484R

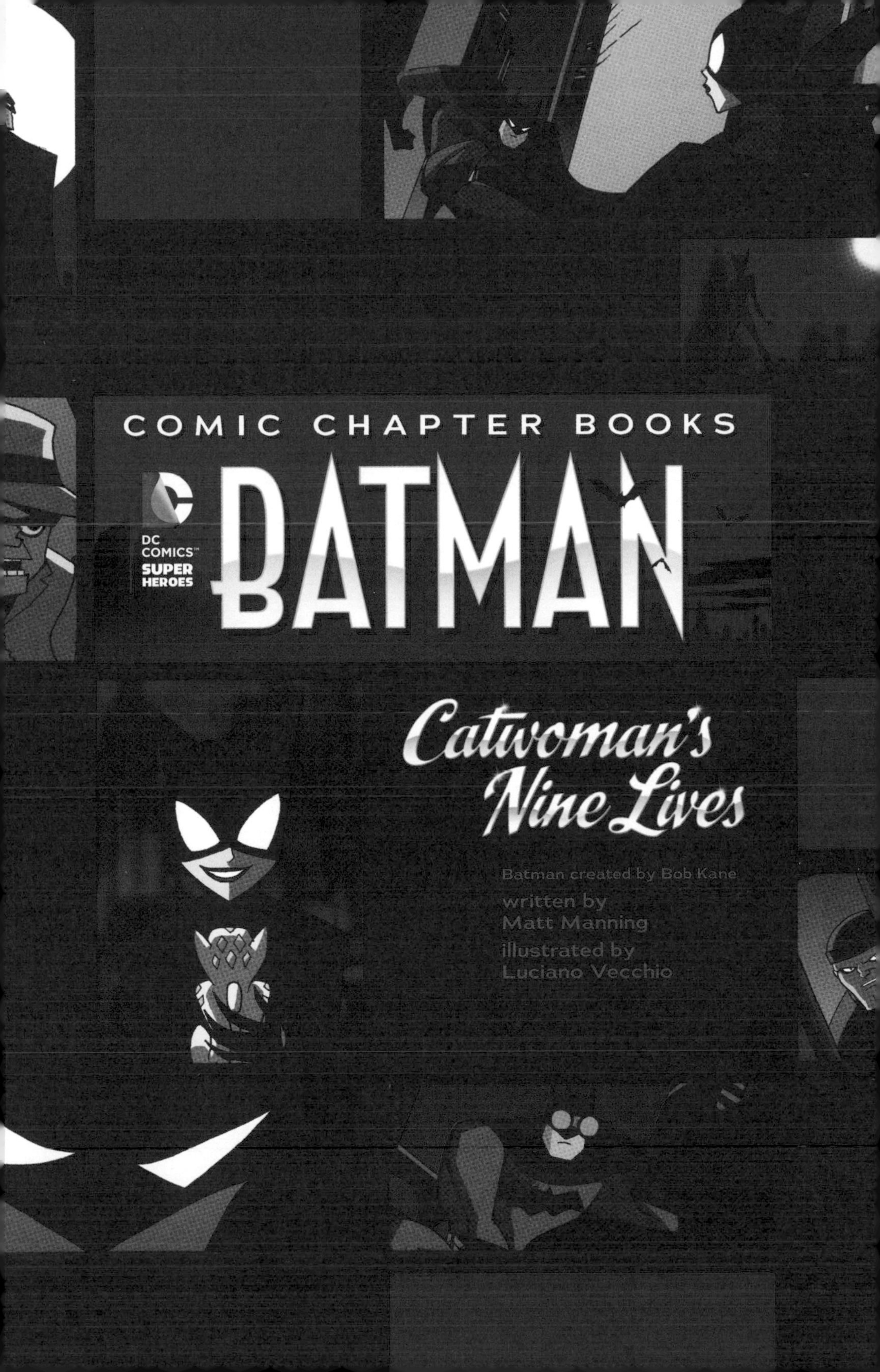

COMIC CHAPTER BOOKS

DC COMICS™ SUPER HEROES

BATMAN

Catwoman's Nine Lives

Batman created by Bob Kane

written by
Matt Manning

illustrated by
Luciano Vecchio

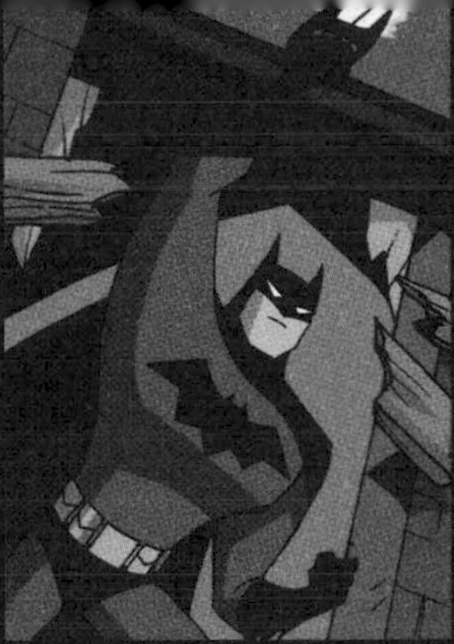

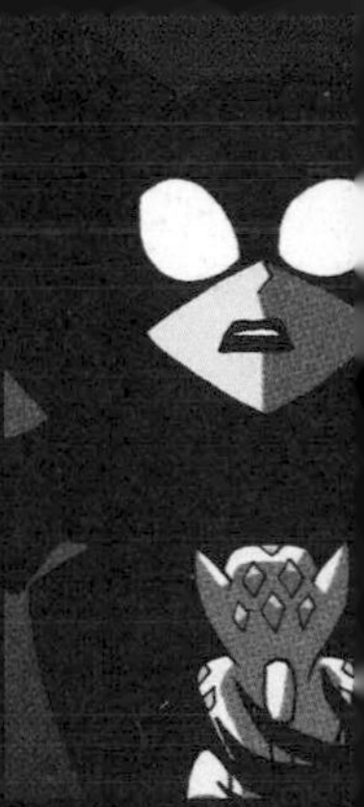

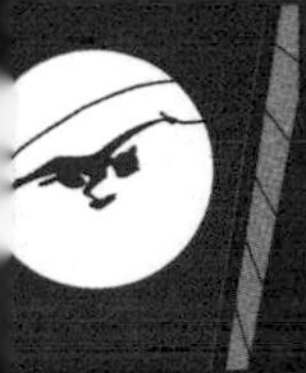

TABLE OF CONTENTS

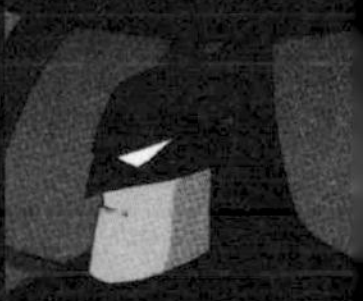

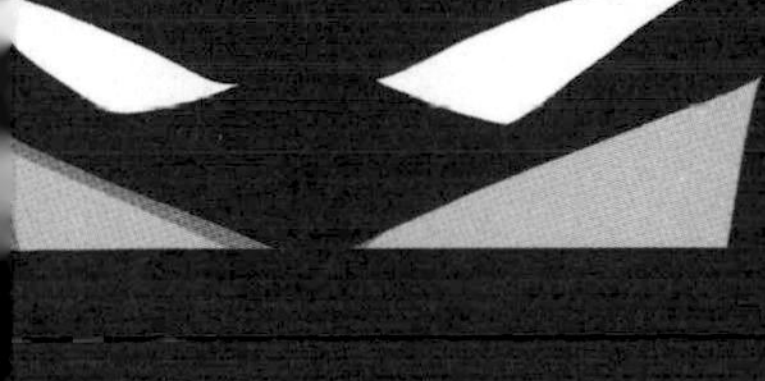

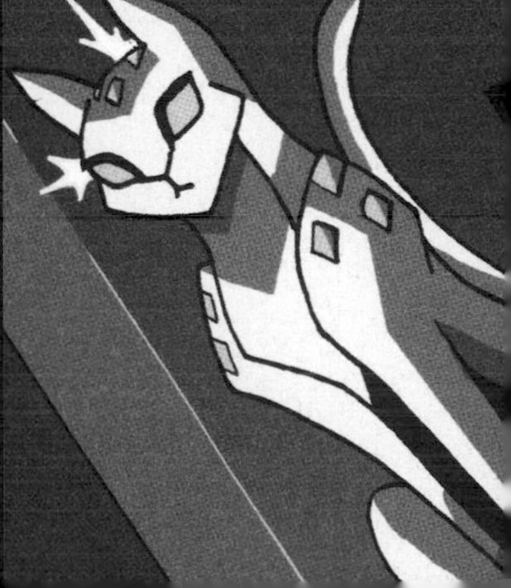

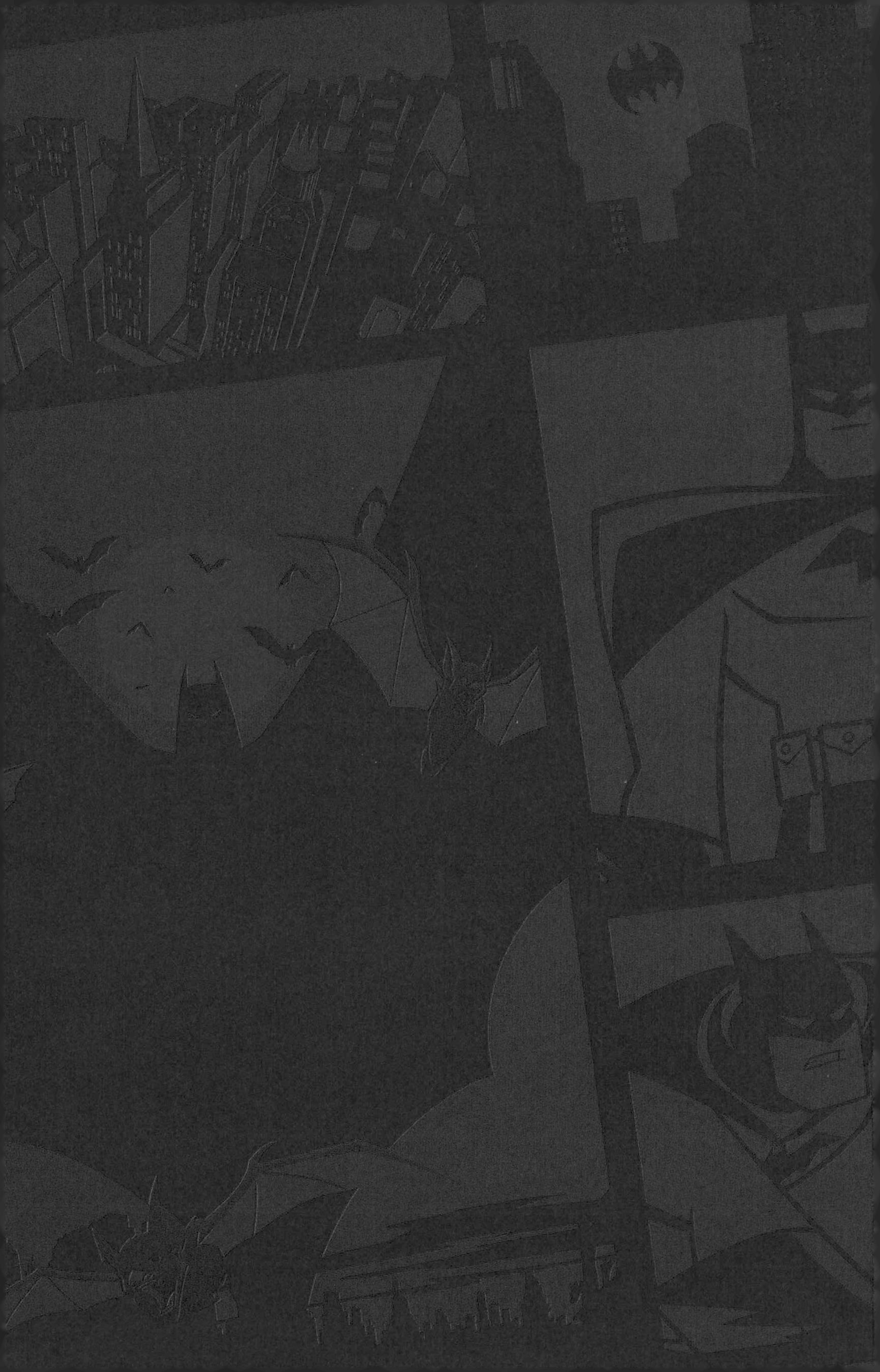

CHAPTER 1

THE PLAYERS

Catwoman loved this type of job. Up on the 37th floor of the Wilshire Point Building, there weren't any drooling guard dogs. There were no glowing red lasers or state-of-the-art motion sensors. For Catwoman, there just wasn't anything difficult about robbing a high-rise apartment.

She inspected the whip tied around her waist. It still held tight. After changing into her costume, she had used it to rappel the short distance from the building's rooftop. Getting into the actual building was easy.

As Selina Kyle, Catwoman never had any trouble with front desk security guards. She'd simply flash a smile and make up an excuse about wanting to surprise a friend who lived there. The guards usually just waved her on by to the elevators. They never saw her as much of a threat. But they never saw her claws . . .

It had been far too long since she had gotten a chance to use those claws. Back when she was working on smaller jobs, Catwoman had to use every tool in the book. But these days, she rarely needed to reach into her bag of tricks to get things done. Take tonight, for example. The window to the 37th-floor penthouse was not only unlocked, but it was also halfway open.

No one living in a high-rise apartment expects a visitor to come calling from the window. In other words, the wealthiest citizens of Gotham City thought their personal ivory towers gave them security. That fact just made it easier for Catwoman to waltz into their living rooms and take whatever she wanted.

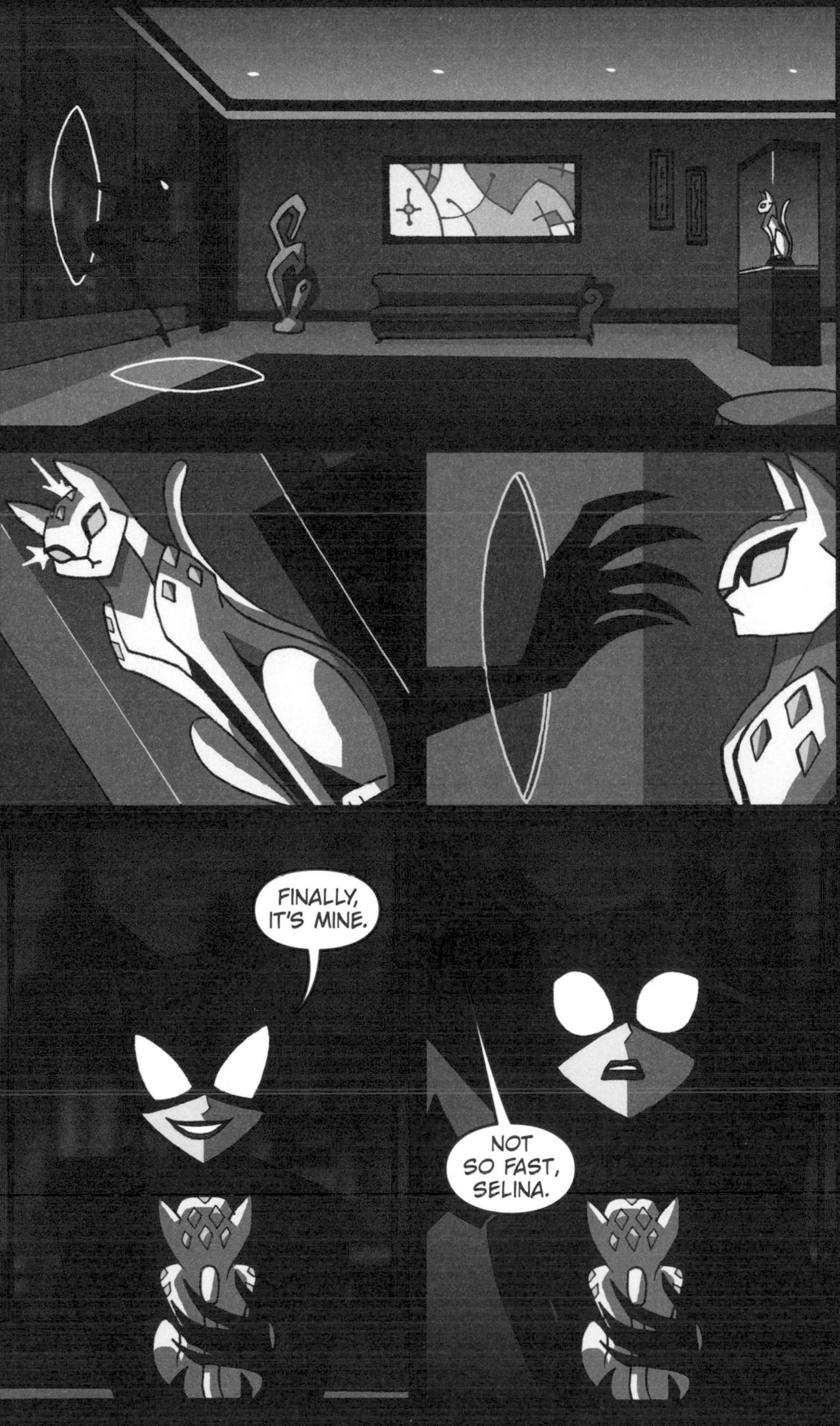
FINALLY, IT'S MINE.
NOT SO FAST, SELINA.

Unfortunately for Catwoman, that sense of false security was contagious and had caused her to drop her guard. The moment she felt the strong hand on her shoulder, she realized who it was. Only one person was capable of sneaking up on her.

While it annoyed her that Batman had interrupted her heist, she couldn't help but smile. Despite the trouble he always caused, Catwoman was always glad to see Batman.

"Put it back, Selina," Batman said.

Instead, Catwoman turned around and faced him, clutching the statue in her hands.

"It's been a while, Batman," Catwoman said. "It seems like you never come around anymore."

"Put it back," Batman repeated. "Or we'll have a problem."

Catwoman began to walk toward the open window. She knew Batman wouldn't stop her quite yet. He'd wait until there was no other choice before acting.

Batman was always hoping Selina would change. He was always giving her the chance to make the right decision. And she was always disappointing him.

"We have plenty of problems already, Batman," she said. "So what's one more problem added to our dysfunctional little relationship?"

"The two of us don't have a relationship," Batman said.

Selina paused at the window then turned around to face Batman again. One of his hands had moved to his Utility Belt near where he kept his Batarangs. That meant one thing: Catwoman had taken this as far as he was willing to let her. If she stepped out the window, she was inviting a fight.

Catwoman chuckled. The scene reminded her of an old-fashioned standoff in a Western movie, only without the guns. In Gotham City, apparently High Noon began at midnight. And Catwoman loved a good showdown.

With a smile and a wink, she backflipped
out the window.

WOOOOOSH!

The heavy night air raced up to meet
Catwoman as she fell. She twisted her body into
a dive. Then she lashed her whip out with her
right hand.

CRACK!

The end of the whip found the head of a
gargoyle and wrapped around it. Suddenly,
Catwoman's fall transformed into a swing. Her
whip released its hold and latched onto another
gargoyle's neck.

CRACK!

She soared from building to building,
searching for a good place to land.

SWOOOOOSH!

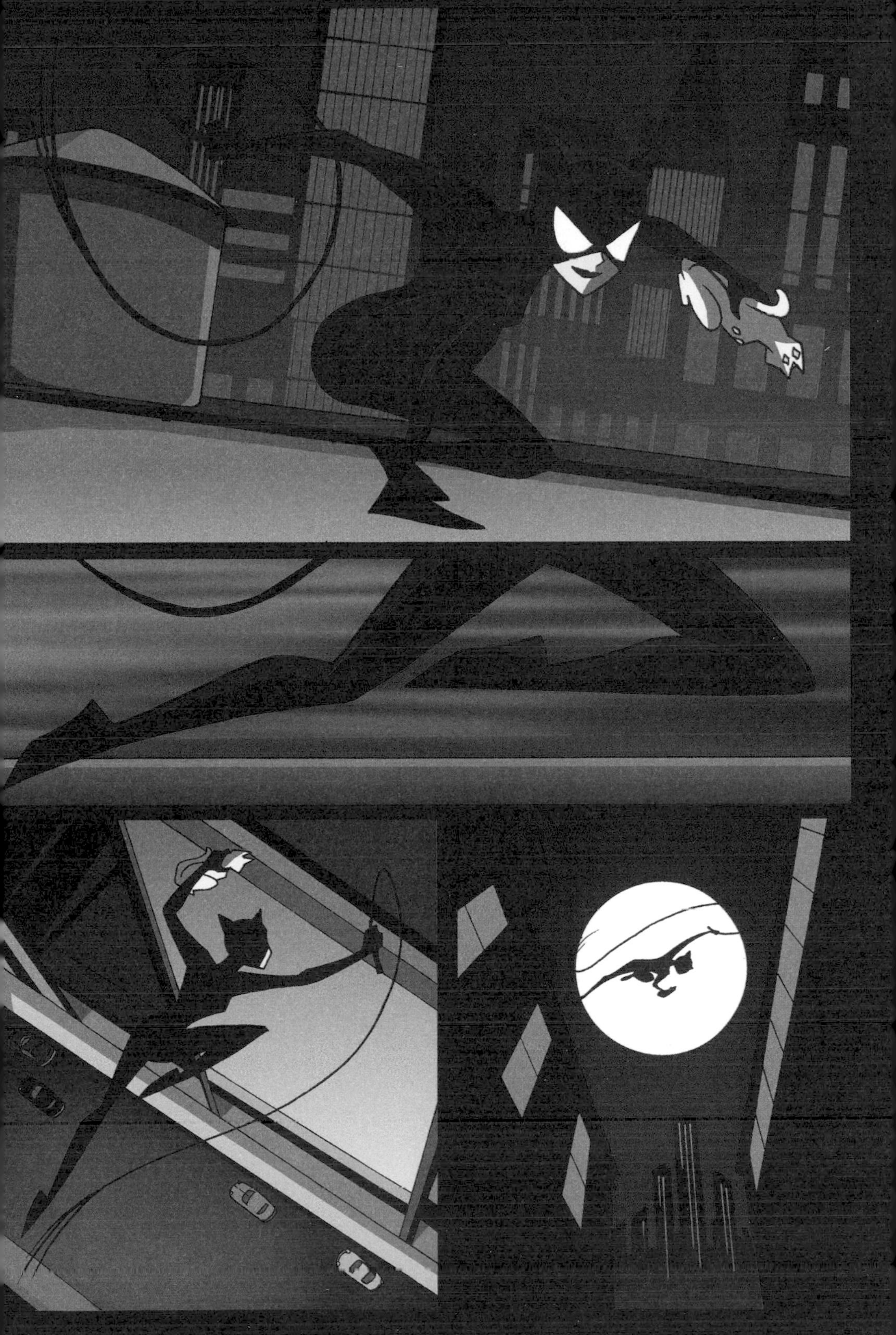

WHUMP!

Catwoman landed softly and immediately began running.

By this point in her career, Catwoman was used to the feel of Gotham City's rooftops beneath her feet. So the loose shingles on the Mayfair building didn't even give her a second's pause. Neither did the smooth finish of the courthouse's ledge.

THUMP THUMP THUMP

And from the sound of the footsteps following her, she knew the same could be said for Batman.

For Selina Kyle, this was as good as it got. The thrill of the chase made her life as Catwoman worthwhile. And while she was intent on ditching Batman, she wasn't in a hurry to see that happen.

After all, this was the fun part.

She jumped from the corner of the courthouse's marble ledge and lashed her whip at the air in front of her.

CRACK!

The whip's tip wrapped around the sign of a florist's storefront, and Catwoman was swinging again. She built up speed as her whip detached from the sign. Before her feet landed on the loose, dried tar of the building across the street, there was a moment of weightlessness. It was like she was a part of the night air itself. She loved that feeling most of all.

THUMP!

But then her feet hit the roof, and she was grounded again. Without looking behind her, Catwoman could tell that Batman was gaining on her. His footsteps were light. They could only be heard with a trained ear, but Catwoman had two of those. He was definitely getting closer. *Too* close.

It was time to end the chase. "It's a good thing I planned for this," she said to herself.

Without slowing down for even a second, Catwoman jumped off another ledge. She aimed her body at a boarded-up window of the third floor of a building across the street. Catwoman curled herself into a tight ball and braced for impact.

CRASH!!

The boards snapped against her weight as she broke into the building. She came to a rolling stop inside the apartment. It was abandoned just like it had been when she inspected it last week. Everything was going according to her plan.

She lashed her whip at the boards on the windows on the other side of the room, and they broke beneath the lash.

CLUNK CLUNK CLUNK

She heard them hitting the ground of the alley behind the building. Quickly, Catwoman ducked into the nearby closet. She held her breath and listened. And waited.

PAT PAT PAT

Even from inside the closet, she heard the quiet padding of Batman's boots in the apartment. By now, he was seeing the broken boards of the window across the room.

PAT PAT CREAK

She could hear him run across the apartment's creaky old floor.

CRACK!

And then she heard another board break as Batman continued out the window. The plan had worked as well as Catwoman had hoped: he thought she'd simply passed through the building without stopping.

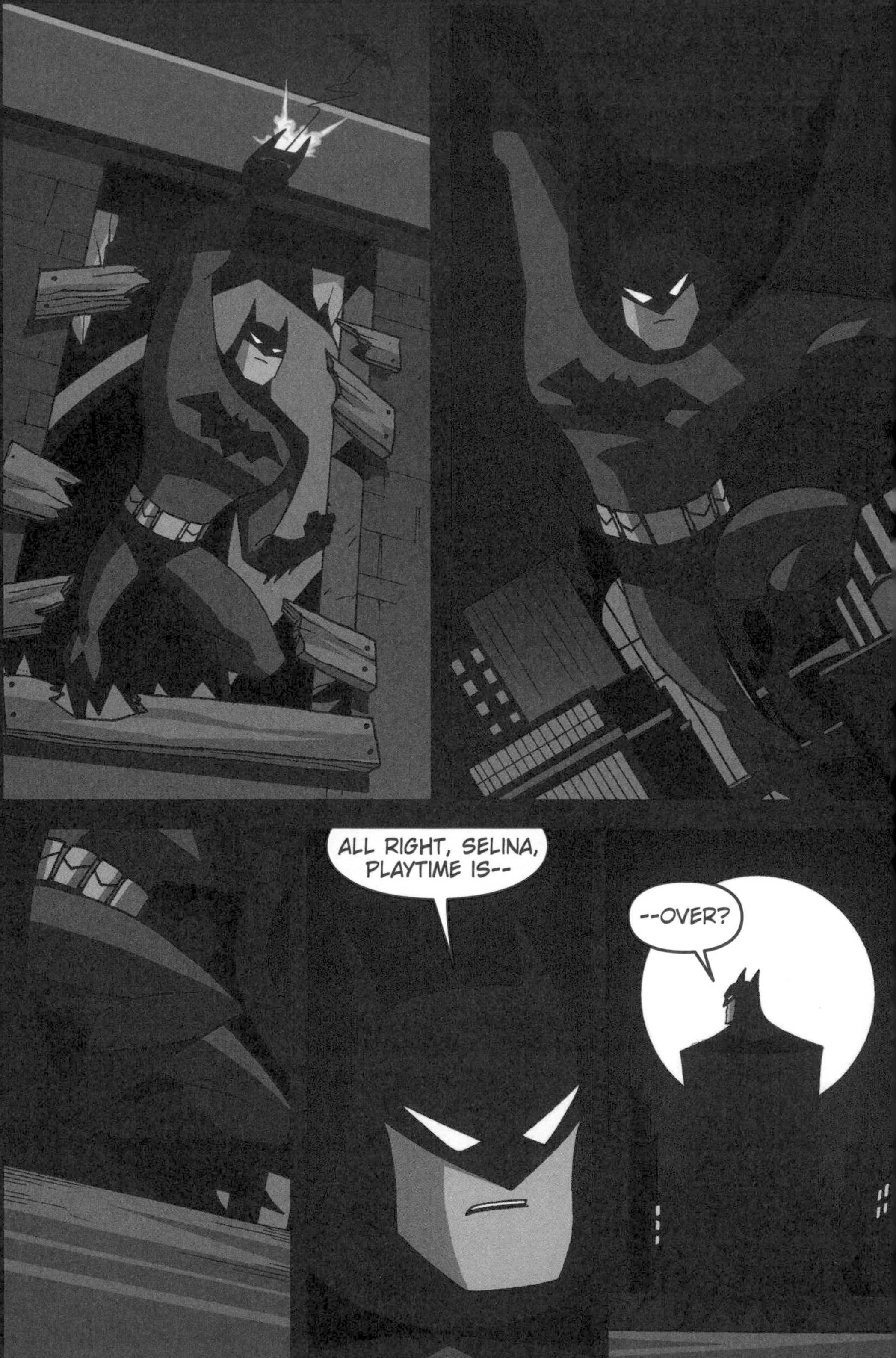
ALL RIGHT, SELINA, PLAYTIME IS--
--OVER?

Catwoman grinned. It wasn't often that someone fooled the Dark Knight, so she was quite pleased with herself. She waited a few moments to make sure he was gone for good.

The closet door didn't make a sound when Catwoman pushed it back open again. Silently, she slid out the window through which she'd originally entered. Then she doubled back the way she had come, making sure to stick to the shadows.

Catwoman took out her whip.

CRACK!

She latched it onto a nearby building and swung to the next one, making her way toward the East End.

A FEW MINNUTES LATER...

Selina arrived at her apartment. As she entered her spacious home through the window lining the fire escape, she saw a shadowy figure waiting for her.

Despite herself, Catwoman smiled again. "Oh, you're good, Batman," she said.

"Oh, I'm not Batman, my dear," a voice said from the darkness. "And you should know that I'm anything but good."

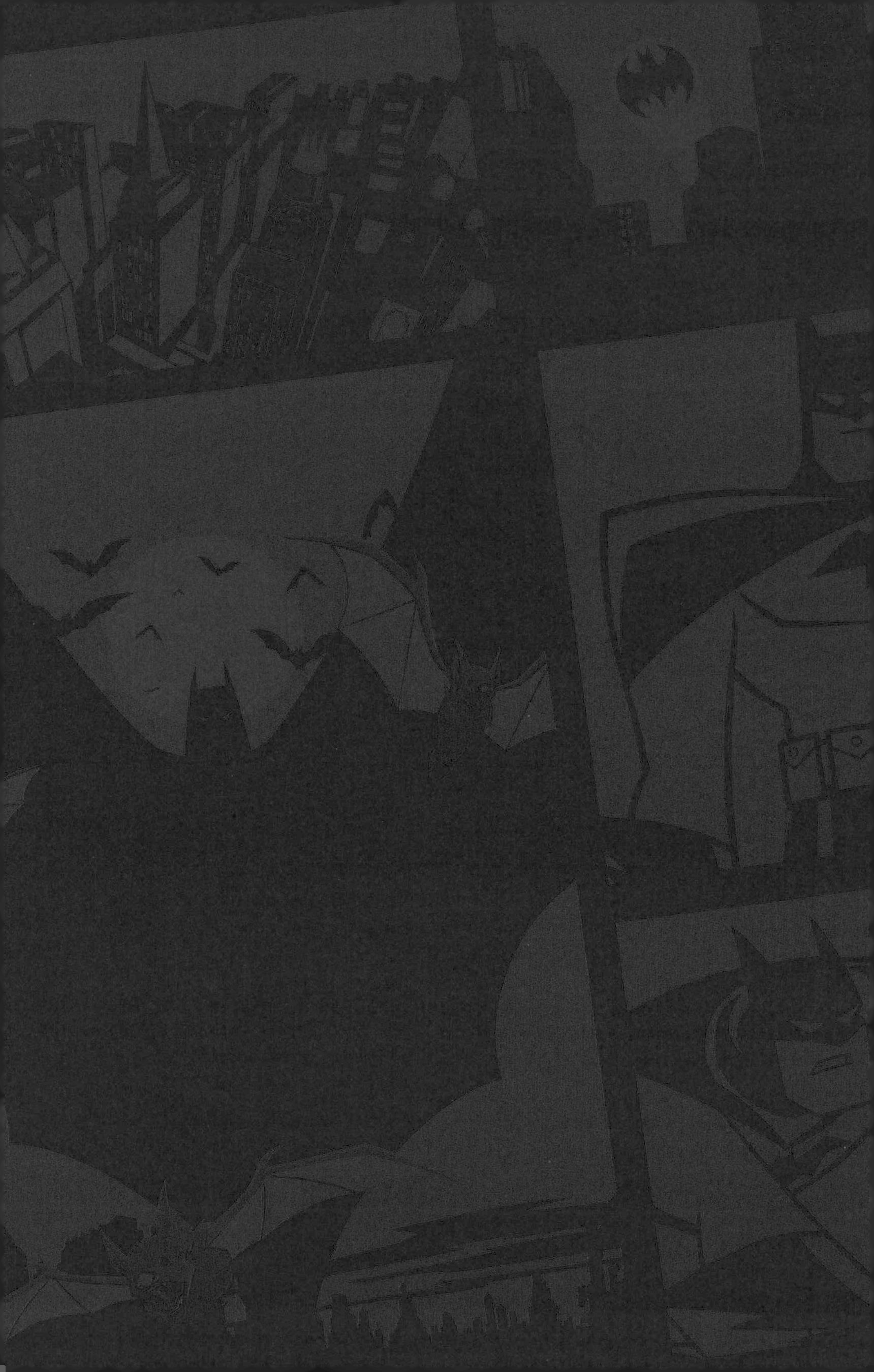

CHAPTER 2

THE TARGET

The Penguin stepped out from the shadows in the corner of the room. Catwoman was honestly surprised how she could ever mistake him for Batman — even in the shadows.

The Penguin was a small man. His clothes were expensive-looking, but they didn't seem to fit quite right. Catwoman knew the Penguin had plenty of money, but for some reason he didn't act like it. There was something strange about this odd little bird-obsessed man. He didn't seem to belong anywhere.

But despite his unimpressive appearance, there was still something very intimidating about the Penguin.

"Penguin,"Catwoman said. "How did you know where to find me?"

"You just answered your own question, young lady," the peculiar man said. "I'm the Penguin. There is very little going on in my city that I'm not aware of."

Catwoman walked across her living room. She carefully placed her new cat statue on the mantle above her fireplace. She took a step back from it and studied it for a moment. Then she repositioned it a bit.

Catwoman turned to face the Penguin. "*Your* city?" she asked. "Some people might disagree with that statement."

"Straight to the point, as always," said the Penguin. "I like that. It's like you know exactly why I'm here."

Catwoman turned back to her newest prized possession.

She used two of her fingers to lovingly stroke the spine of her valuable cat statue. It was like she was stroking its fur. It was her newest toy. Her pet. Even the Penguin wasn't going to ruin her enjoyment.

"Go on and spit it out," Catwoman said. "I'm a busy feline."

"Now you're bordering on rude," said the Penguin. He took a seat on Catwoman's couch. "I'd be more respectful if I were you."

Catwoman turned to look at him again. "Am I on thin ice?" she purred.

"Ha," said Penguin. "Okay, you've won back my favor. I guess I'm a pushover." He cleared his throat. "In any event, I'd like to tell you a little story."

Catwoman felt the weight of her whip at her side. It was there if she ended up needing it. From the way the Penguin was acting, she didn't think she would. He seemed to need her for some reason. It only made sense to let him tell her why.

Catwoman nodded for him to continue. "Good. As you know, I'm a bit of a mover and a shaker here in Gotham City," the Penguin said. I run crime, or crime doesn't run at all. But lately, I've been getting some competition from one of my, shall we say, ambitious peers. I'd like that competition to stop."

The Penguin stood up again. He walked over to Catwoman and fixed his eyes on hers. "The Ventriloquist thinks he can run the Gotham City mob better than I can," the Penguin said. "So I want him eliminated from the game."

Catwoman's hand tightened on her whip. "I don't kill," she said.

"My dear, I'm not the kind of man to ask for orange juice at a lemonade stand," the Penguin said through his smile. The room was dark, but his yellowed teeth were still visible to Catwoman. "You're a thief. So I'm asking you to do what you're good at. The Ventriloquist isn't quite right in the head — that's no secret. He gets all his advice from his puppet, Scarface."

The Penguin took a few steps closer to her. "So, my little cat burglar, I want to pay you to steal the dummy's dummy."

Catwoman paused for a second. Then she took a few steps closer to the Penguin. When she was about a foot away from him, she stopped and looked down into the strange little man's face. His eyes were as yellow as his smile.

"And what if I say no?" she asked.

The Penguin's grin stretched from ear to ear. "Now why would you do that?" he said. He walked past Catwoman and focused his gaze on the cat statue on her mantle. "The way I see it, it'd be much easier to get your claws on pretty little kitties like this one with cash instead of thievery."

Catwoman grinned. "Why would I buy them," she said, "when I have so much more fun stealing them?"

The Penguin turned to face her so quickly that her hand instinctively went to her whip. "Precisely," he said, his eyes fixed on hers.

"And that's exactly why you're the perfect cat for this task," the Penguin added. "You enjoy stealing, you're quite good at it, and you could use the cold, hard cash."

Catwoman smiled. She couldn't help but appreciate how good the Penguin was with words. He had basically trapped her into saying yes with his quick thinking and silver tongue. Not that she minded much. A job was a job, and even a cat needs to pay the bills.

"I'm in," she said.

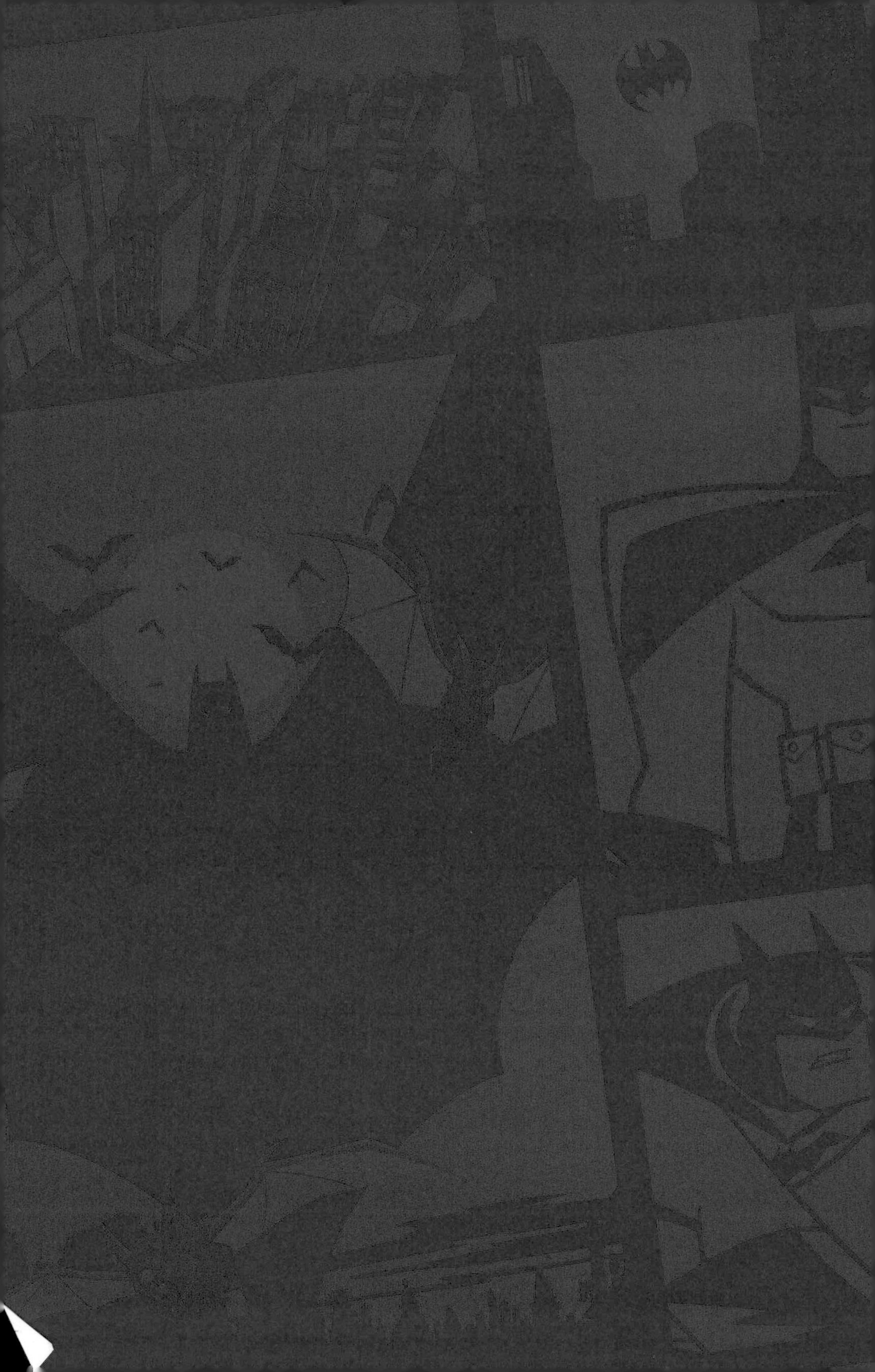

CHAPTER 3

THE HEIST

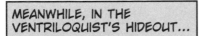

MEANWHILE, IN THE
VENTRILOQUIST'S HIDEOUT...

SCRAPE. SCRAPE.

"Careful, Carl," said the puppet. "You think I want a matching pair?"

The large mountain of a man called Carl wasn't quite sure what his boss was talking about. So he stopped what he was doing and straightened himself up. He looked down at the wooden ventriloquist dummy sitting on the barber's chair in front of him.

The puppet looked pretty silly there all by itself. Its head was cocked to one side and was half covered in shaving cream.

Carl wiped the shaving cream off the razor in his hand. "What ya mean by 'matching pair,' Mr. Scarface?" he asked.

"I already got one scar," the puppet seemed to say. "I don't need a second one."

"Oh, gotcha," Carl said. Then he bent back over and began shaving Scarface's face again.

Deep down, Carl knew that what he was doing was ridiculous. He knew that Scarface wasn't alive. Currently, the puppet wasn't even moving when it talked. But the voice coming from it was convincing. The Ventriloquist made it all seem believable. Sometimes it was hard to remember that his boss wasn't this imposing wooden toy in front of him but actually the small, nervous man sitting behind him.

Near the door, the Ventriloquist sat, apparently reading the evening's paper. He looked casual. Relaxed.

An outside observer would think the Ventriloquist wasn't even paying attention to the strange scene in front of him. But he was always watching. And listening.

"Ya' seeing what this guy's doing, Dummy?" Scarface called to his puppeteer.

The Ventriloquist put down his paper. "I . . . I'm sorry, Mr. Scarface," he said. "I was trying to catch up on the, um, news."

"You can search the personals on your own time," the puppet seemed to say. "You're on the clock, Dummy."

"S-sorry, sorry," the Ventriloquist whined.

"'Sorry, sorry,'" Scarface said in a mocking tone. "Shut up, ya mook."

Carl looked down at the limp wooden toy in front of him. He knew the Ventriloquist was arguing with himself, but it didn't make Scarface any less intimidating. He wiped the puppet's face with a towel. "Finished, boss," he said.

"You're right you're finished," said Scarface. "You're lucky you're not finished for good, the way you shave."

"Mr. Scarface —" Carl started to say.

"No, you know what?" the dummy said. "Get out of here, the lot of yas. Leave me alone. I need to get some thinking done, and you twos won't shut yer traps."

The Ventriloquist stood up. He looked as if he was about to speak. Then he thought better of it, put his head down, and shuffled out of the room.

"You too, doofus!" Scarface shouted.

Carl put his razor blade in the cup of water on the desk near Scarface's chair. He wiped his hands quickly on the towel. He smiled at the puppet that he knew couldn't actually see him, then he left the room.

Neither the Ventriloquist nor Carl saw the shadowy figure above them as she descended through the room's skylight. She, too, had a big smile on her face.

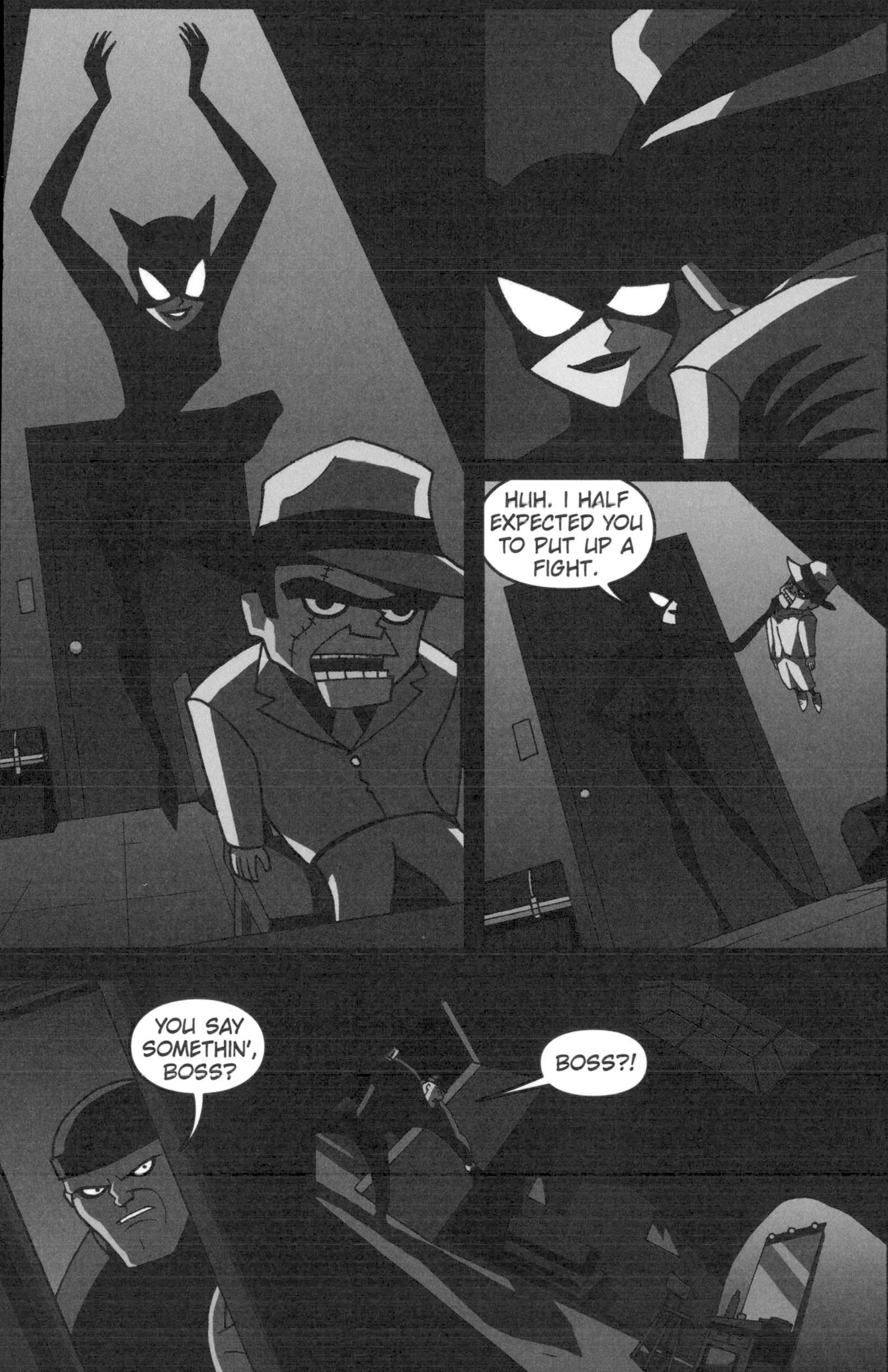
HUH. I HALF EXPECTED YOU TO PUT UP A FIGHT.
YOU SAY SOMETHIN', BOSS?
BOSS?!

Batman adjusted the black metal device on the window pane. He pressed the switch on its side to activate it. Then he pushed himself back up to his feet, using the rooftop's ledge for support. Batman tapped a finger on his cowl above his ear.

CRACKLE-KRRZZZT!

There was a split second of feedback that caught him by surprise. He took a step back from the ledge of the rooftop, and the feedback stopped. Now all he could hear were the voices in the building below him.

"I'm not sure what we can do," a voice was saying.

Batman immediately recognized the nervous, high-strung voice of Arnold Wesker, the Ventriloquist.

"This isn't my job. I don't —"

SKREEEEEEEE!

A loud ringing filled Batman's cowl. He tapped above his ear twice, and the sound softened. In the building below him, the Ventriloquist's phone was ringing.

Batman touched a different part of his cowl. It activated a direct link to the Ventriloquist's phone, taking full advantage of the tap he'd planted on the criminal's line earlier.

"Hello?" the Ventriloquist said.

"Wesker," said the man on the phone. He wasn't asking. He knew exactly whom he was speaking to.

"That's . . . that's right," the Ventriloquist stammered.

"You know who this is, don't you?" the man on the phone said.

"Yes," said the Ventriloquist.

Batman recognized who it was, too. The Penguin's voice was one he knew all too well.

"Then you should know that I don't make empty threats," said the Penguin.

The Ventriloquist didn't respond.

"I have your little friend," the Penguin said.

"My little — Mr. Scarface?!" said the Ventriloquist, his voice shaking as he realized what was happening. "Don't you hurt him!" he yelled into the phone.

"He's fine, he's fine," said the Penguin. "Don't ruffle your feathers. But if you want him to stay that way, meet me tomorrow at Pier 58. You'll get Scarface back, but in exchange . . . both of you must leave Gotham City for good."

"But Mr. Scarface won't —" the Ventriloquist started to say.

"Mr. Scarface will do what I tell him to do if he wants to live," said the Penguin. "Pier 58. Tomorrow at midnight. Come alone."

CLICK

The line went silent. Batman raised his hand to his cowl, ready to turn the phone tap off. But then the Ventriloquist spoke again.

"Hello?" he said into the dead phone. "Is somebody there?"

"It's me, you Dummy," said another voice. It was harsh and grating. Batman recognized it. It was the voice of Scarface.

CLICK CLICK CLICK

Batman tapped his earpiece three times so that his cowl would begin to record the conversation. He didn't want to miss a word of what he was hearing.

"Mr. Scarface!" the Ventriloquist exclaimed. "You're alive!"

"Of course I'm alive," said Scarface. "I managed to slip away from the Penguin's goons for a second."

"Sir, I'm —" the Ventriloquist began.

"Shut your mouth, Dummy," said Scarface. "I need ya to listen to me and you better listen real good. I don't have much time before they get back here."

The conversation was insane — and interesting — to Batman at the same time. The Ventriloquist was talking to himself. But his mind was so far gone that he wasn't even aware of the fact that it was a one-sided conversation.

"The Penguin wants us to skip town, right?" said Scarface. "But we're gonna do the opposite. I got other plans for that feathered felon."

"Sir?" Wesker asked quietly.

"You might want to get a pen and paper, Dummy," said Scarface. "I don't want to have to repeat all this later."

LATER THAT NIGHT...

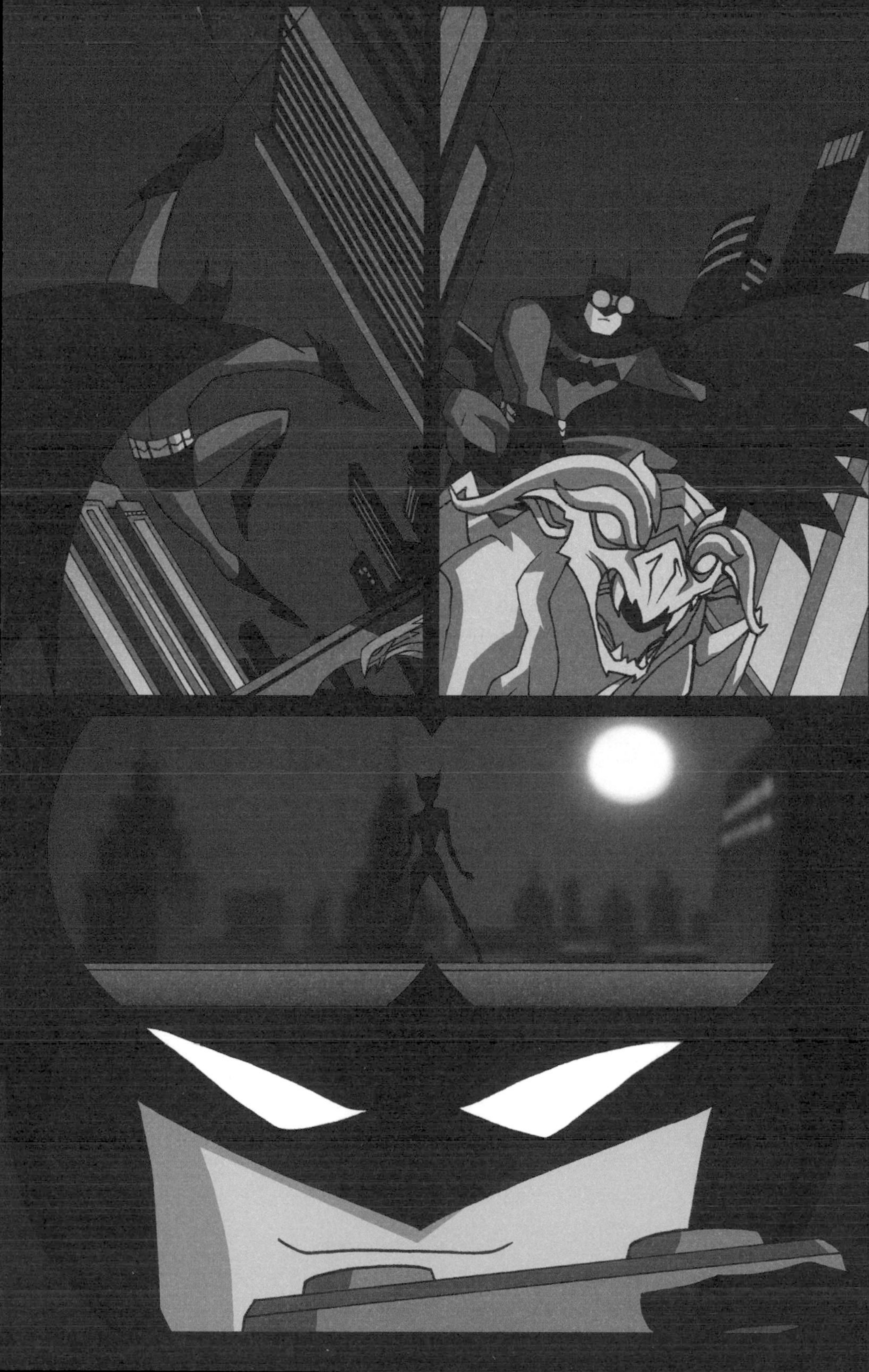

"Gotcha," Batman said.

The Dark Knight slipped back into the shadows, pocketed his binoculars, and waited.

Soon enough, Catwoman was on the move. "You won't sneak away from me this time," Batman said.

Sticking to the shadows, Batman followed Catwoman. He took great care not to get too close too quickly. Carelessness had gotten the better of him last time he'd chased after her.

That would not happen again.

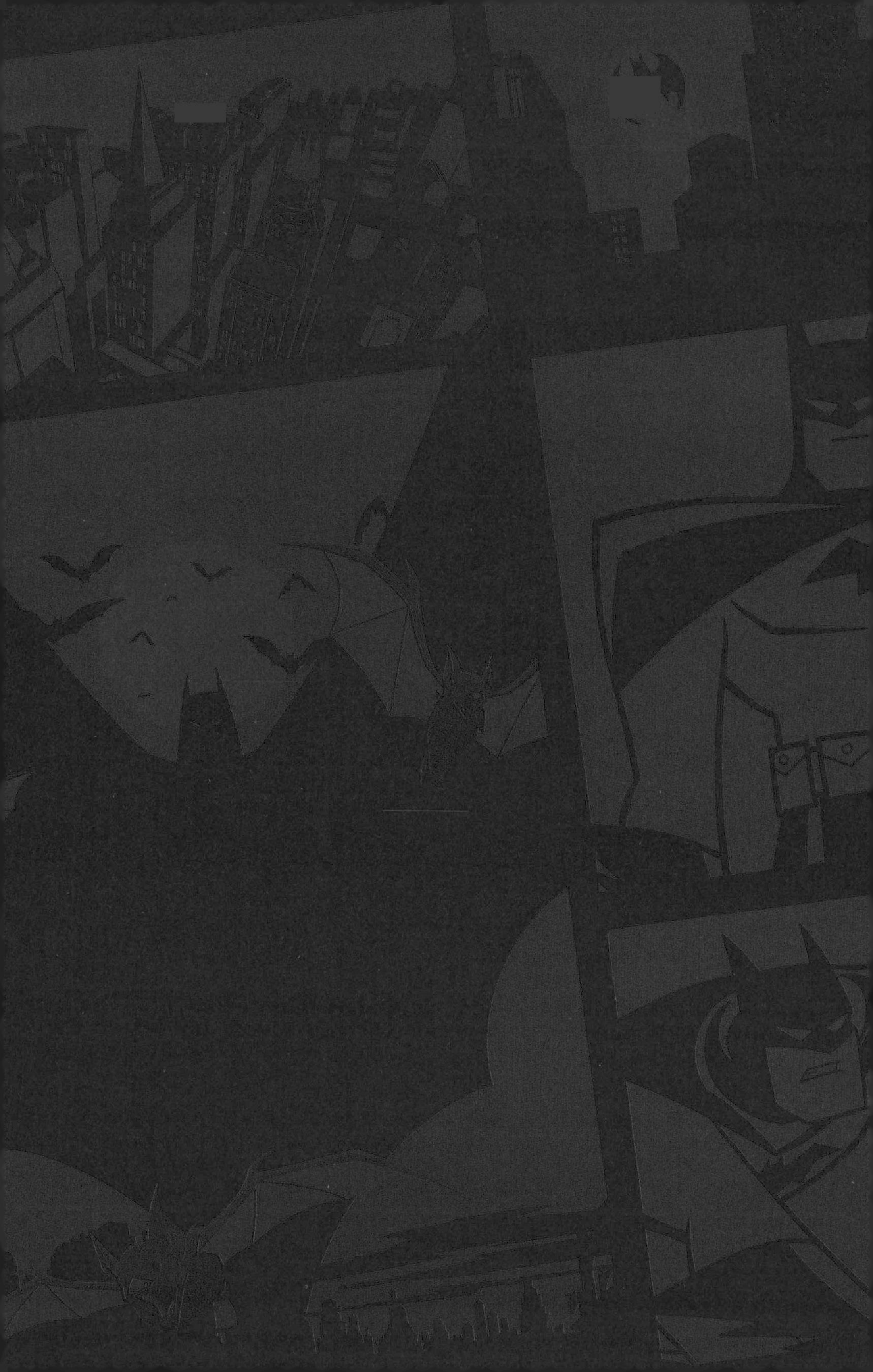

CHAPTER 4
THE PARTNERSHIP

It had taken Batman the better part of the evening, but he eventually managed to catch up to Catwoman. He was actually surprised that it hadn't taken longer. Catwoman was usually much faster and more elusive.

He continued his cautious, quiet approach as he neared her. When it came to Selina Kyle, Batman never knew exactly how she was going to react. But he was pretty sure that after their encounter last night, she wouldn't exactly be happy to see him.

Catwoman stood perched on the ledge of the rooftop. Batman wasn't sure what she was doing. Perhaps staking out a new target? He had always found it difficult to get into Selina's head. She was a mystery to him — more so than the other criminals he chased. Regardless of the reason, Selina never seemed to be far from Batman's thoughts.

Batman moved quietly across the roof. Catwoman wouldn't be able to hear his footsteps. At least that's what he thought.

But when Batman stepped a bit closer, Catwoman straightened up and rolled her shoulders forward a little. That meant one of two things: she was either getting ready for a fight, or she was just getting ready to run.

Batman reached into his Utility Belt.

CLICK.

As quietly as possible, Batman produced a Batarang with a wire attached to it. He prepared himself for anything.

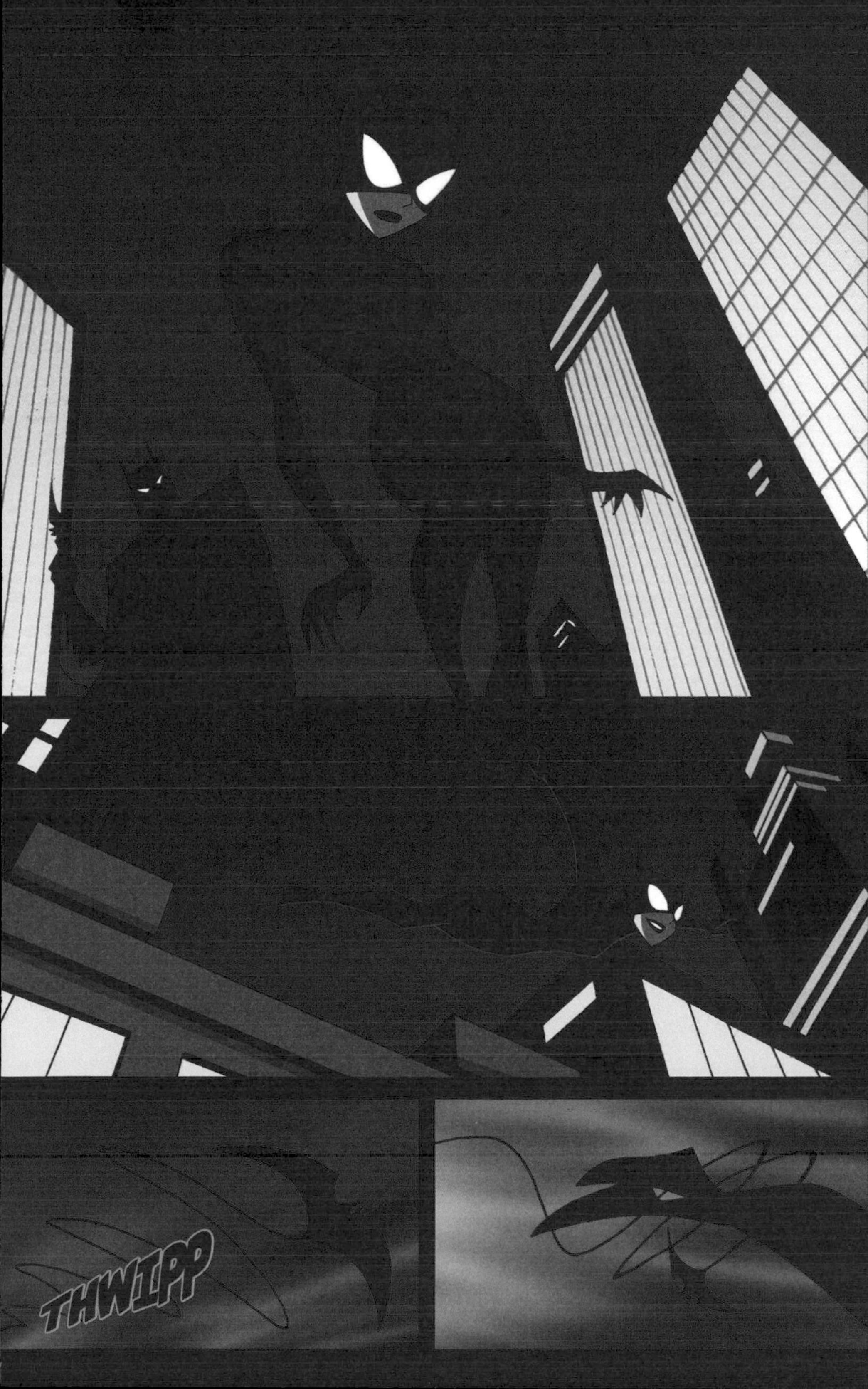
THWIPP

TWANG!

Luckily for Batman, his aim was as good as ever. He couldn't even count how many hours of mind-numbing target practice he'd put in back at the Batcave with his Batarangs. But it proved worth the effort on this night.

Batman made his way to the building's ledge. Now it would just be a simple matter of reeling her back up to the rooftop. They needed to have a serious talk. And Batman had to be sure that she wasn't going to depart in the middle of their conversation.

But in the three seconds it took Batman to cross the roof, Catwoman had already sliced his line and was running into an alley down on the street below.

There was always a chase when it came to Catwoman. Without thinking twice, Batman jumped over the ledge and shot his grapnel.

FWOOM!

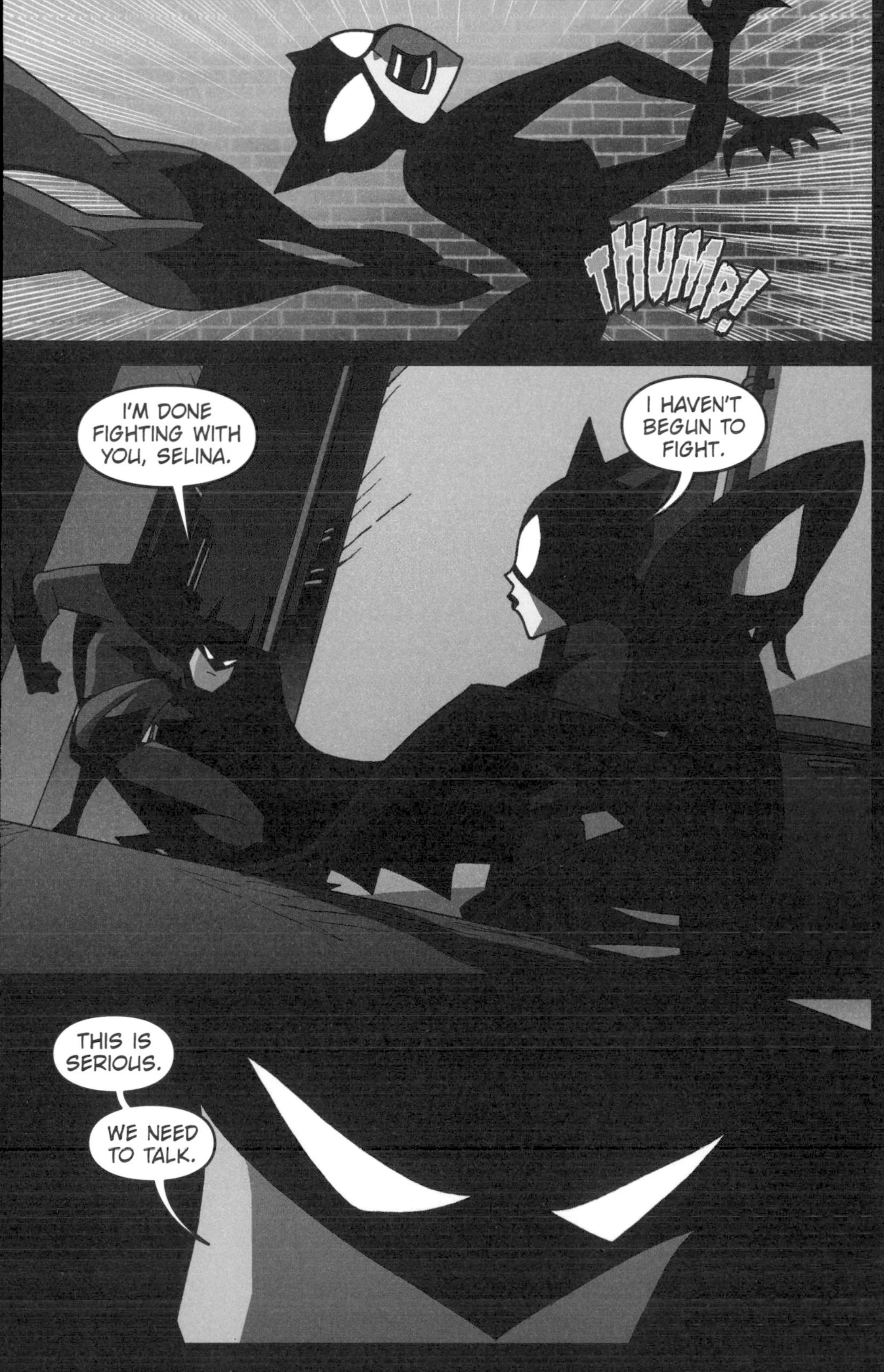
THUMP!
I'M DONE FIGHTING WITH YOU, SELINA.
I HAVEN'T BEGUN TO FIGHT.
THIS IS SERIOUS.
WE NEED TO TALK.

Catwoman knew Batman well enough to know that he meant what he'd just said. And Batman was counting on that fact. But just in case Catwoman tried something, he kept one hand on his Utility Belt as they climbed the fire escape back to the rooftop.

When they reached the roof, Batman let Catwoman take a few steps away from him. The Dark Knight wanted her to think that she was in control of the situation. Catwoman was only comfortable when she felt like she was the one in control.

"What do you want from me, Batman?" she asked.

"You stole Scarface from the Ventriloquist," said Batman. "Because of your actions, things are about to get messy. You will be partly responsible for any bloodshed that follows."

"As long as the Penguin transfers me the money he promised, I'm not really concerned," said Catwoman.

"I thought you didn't kill," Batman said.

Batman took a step closer to her. "Isn't that what makes you different from the Penguin and the Ventriloquist?" he asked.

"I haven't killed anyone," she said.

"Not yet," said Batman. "But tomorrow at midnight, the Ventriloquist plans to ambush the Penguin at their meeting. He has no intention of leaving town. In fact, he's hired every hit man, thug, and criminal he could find. He plans to wipe out the Penguin and his entire crew as soon as Scarface is back in his nervous little hands."

Catwoman narrowed her eyes. "That has nothing to do with me," she said. She walked over to the side of the rooftop.

Batman took his hand away from his Utility Belt. He could read her body language this time. It was clear that she wasn't going to try to run away.

"So what do you want me to do?" Catwoman asked, her back still to Batman.

Batman smiled. "I need a thief."

Catwoman turned to look at him. The slightly sad look on her face told the whole story. She was offering her help without saying a single word.

"The two of us are going to steal back Scarface," Batman said.

"I kind of had the feeling that would be the case," Catwoman grumbled.

CHAPTER 5

THE MEET

A LITTLE BEFORE MIDNIGHT...

There were very few things the Penguin liked in life. Money was one of them. Power was another. He was even quite fond of fear — when he wasn't the one experiencing it, anyway. But the Penguin hated almost everything else.

He especially hated waiting. And cramped quarters. And when things didn't go exactly like he wanted them to.

So when the Penguin's limo stopped in the middle of Pine Boulevard, the Penguin was immediately angry.

"What's the hold up?" the Penguin yelled up to his driver. The Penguin leaned forward on his seat, lifting his arm off the large suitcase next to him.

"Looks like the cops," the driver said back to him. "Some kind of checkpoint, I think."

The Penguin looked at his three bodyguards sitting across from him. None of them jumped into action. That was another thing the Penguin hated: having to tell people how to do their jobs. "Well, what are you waiting for? Get out there and see what's going on!"

The three lumbering bodyguards climbed out of the limo and stood on guard on the Gotham City street.

"What are you three doing?" a man's voice said. "This is a security checkpoint. Do not leave your vehicles!"

The three bodyguards looked at each other and then hesitated at the open door of the limo. They weren't quite sure what to do. The officer walking over to them was a large man. He didn't seem very pleasant. But the Penguin was far worse.

The Penguin popped his head out of the door. "What's the meaning of this?" he cried.

The officer stood in front of the Penguin's bodyguards now. "Is this your boss?" he asked them. Before they could answer, he turned to the Penguin and said, "Are you their boss?"

"That's right," said the Penguin. "I'm in charge here."

CLICK!

The Penguin heard a noise behind him. He turned around to see a policewoman looking inside the back of the limo from the other door. She began to look around the backseat in what seemed to be a routine police inspection.

"Close that door!" the Penguin yelled. Then he turned back to the officer outside his own door. "Tell her to close that door!"

"I'd like it if you didn't tell my partner how to do her job," the policeman said. "In fact, why don't you step out of the vehicle for me?"

"I will do no such thing," said the Penguin. "Do you know who I am?"

The expression on the policeman's face told the Penguin that not only did the officer not know who he was, but he didn't care one way or the other. What the officer did seem to know was how much bigger he was than the Penguin.

So the little bird man thought over his options for a moment. Then he stepped out of the car. A series of questions from the policeman followed.

"You seem to be in a hurry this evening."

"I'm not."

"Well where are you headed?"

"Visiting my mother."

"Has anyone in your party been drinking alcoholic beverages?"

"No. I don't let my men drink while they're on the clock."

"Do you have any illegal weapons of any kind on your person?"

The Penguin sighed. "No."

A dozen more questions followed, and the Penguin answered them similarly. It didn't matter if he was lying or not. He just wanted the interrogation to be over. This sort of thing was beneath him. He wasn't supposed to be the type of person that had to stop at random police checkpoints. And he had a meeting with the Ventriloquist to get to.

Finally, the officers allowed the Penguin and his bodyguards to get back inside the limo. As the policewoman flagged them on, the Penguin rested his arm back on the suitcase on the seat next to him.

But for some reason, he just couldn't seem to get comfortable.

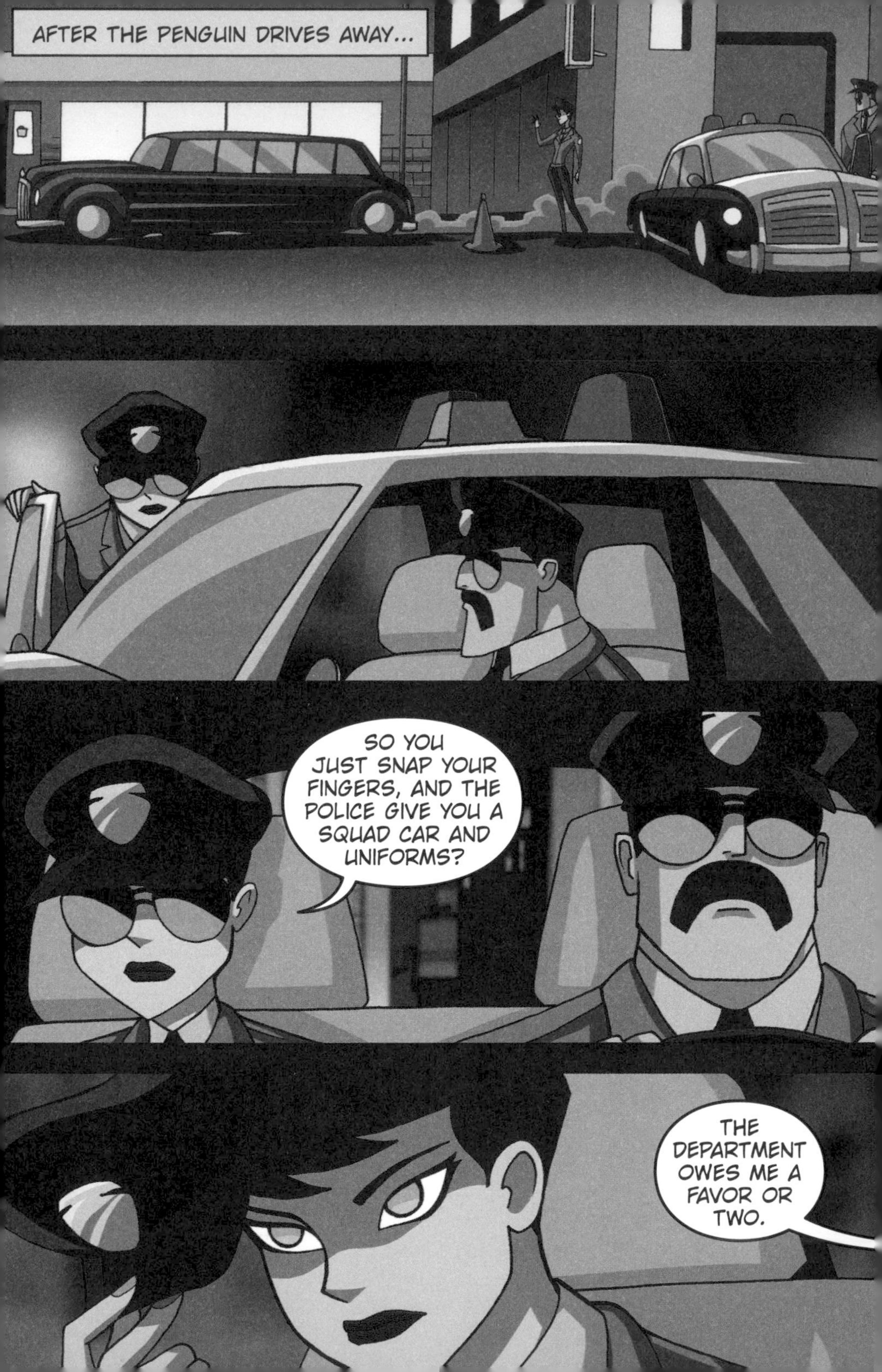
AFTER THE PENGUIN DRIVES AWAY...
SO YOU JUST SNAP YOUR FINGERS, AND THE POLICE GIVE YOU A SQUAD CAR AND UNIFORMS?
THE DEPARTMENT OWES ME A FAVOR OR TWO.

"Did you make the switch?" Batman asked.

"The suitcase is in the back," Selina said. "He didn't see it happen." She smirked. "You know, the two of us really do make a good team."

Selina waited for a response. "What do you think, Batman?" she asked.

When he didn't answer, Selina glanced over her shoulder. She was now alone in the car. The door was open, and a policeman's hat and mustache were resting on the back seat.

MEANWHILE...

TAP-TAP. TAP-TAP.

The Ventriloquist nervously paced across the wooden planks at the end of Pier 58. The Penguin was twenty minutes late. It made the Ventriloquist worry that this plan wasn't going to work. He looked at the large boat anchored at the right of the dock. Then he looked at the boat on the dock's opposite side.

The Ventriloquist sighed. He needed Mr. Scarface back. He just didn't know what to do without him.

Wesker fished his phone out of his pocket and thumbed the display. No missed calls. No messages. The Ventriloquist put the phone back in his pocket and began to pace across the dock's wooden planks again.

Two steps later, the bright lights of a limo flashed over the Ventriloquist's glasses. He steeled himself. This talk had to go well. He needed to do his very best impression of Mr. Scarface.

"Sorry we're late," the Penguin said as he stepped out the side door of the long black car. "Had some trouble with the police, believe it or not."

The Ventriloquist looked at the Penguin's hand. He was carrying some sort of suitcase that was large enough to hold Mr. Scarface. The Ventriloquist heard himself make a quiet whimper. Then he straightened himself.

That's no way for a crime boss to behave. He had to get his act together. He was doing this for Mr. Scarface.

"Is that him?" the Ventriloquist said. He was pretty sure he heard his voice crack when he spoke. He just hoped the Penguin hadn't.

"That's right," said the Penguin as he put the case down on the dock. "All packed up and ready to get out of town."

"A deal is a deal," said the Ventriloquist. "Just give me back Mr. Scarface."

The Penguin smiled. Then he waved his gloved white hand. The Ventriloquist watched as three large bodyguards stepped out of the limo and walked behind their boss. The largest of the three picked up the suitcase. He walked over to the Ventriloquist. The goon set the case down in front of the Ventriloquist.

There was no need to play it cool any longer. Wesker immediately fell to his knees and unzipped the suitcase.

ZZZZZZZZIP!

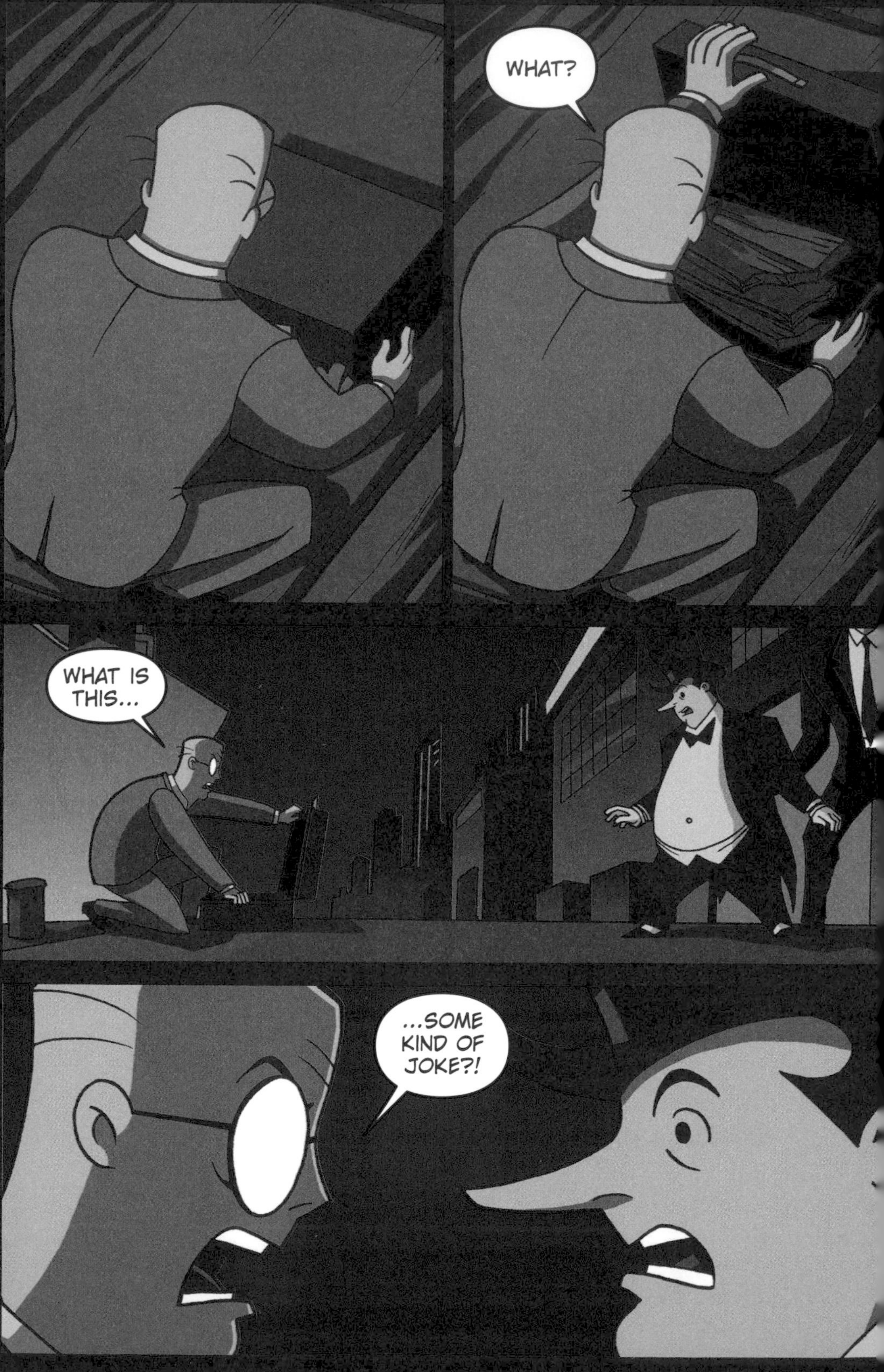
WHAT?
WHAT IS THIS...
...SOME KIND OF JOKE?!

Mr. Scarface wasn't in the suitcase — that much was clear. The Ventriloquist didn't really care why at that point. And he wasn't interested in hearing the Penguin's excuses.

Something had snapped inside Arnold Wesker. In that moment, he realized that he was much more like Mr. Scarface than he ever gave himself credit for.

"Um," was all the Penguin could say. He took a step backward, nodding at his bodyguards to pull out their weapons.

The Ventriloquist had a particularly sinister scowl on his face. "Don't make me hurt you," he warned, wagging his finger.

The Penguin attempted to gather his composure. After all, Wesker was as harmless as a fly without Scarface by his side. And he was outnumbered four to one here, too. The fool had come alone.

The Penguin smirked. "You and what army, tough guy?" he mocked.

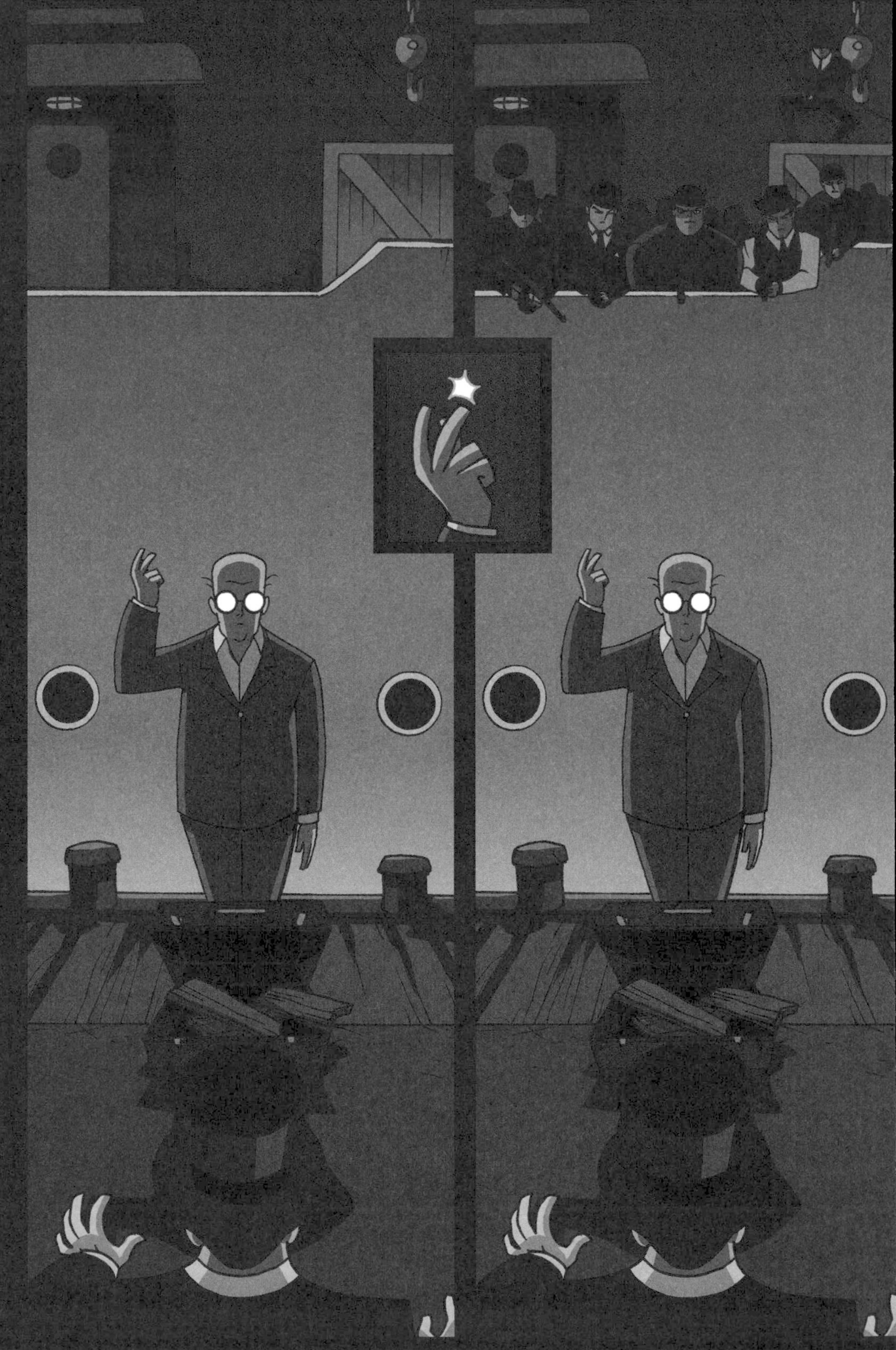

The Penguin had been doing what he does long enough to realize when he was in a no-win situation. There were so many thugs holding weapons staring at him that he knew he couldn't escape. The Ventriloquist had him completely surrounded.

Of course, that didn't stop the Penguin from trying to save his own skin. "Wesker, listen, there's been some sort of mistake," he said.

"No, you came here unprepared," said the Ventriloquist. "You didn't think I had this in me, did you?"

"Well, no," said the Penguin. "If we're being honest, I didn't. But let's not fly off the handle without thinking this thing through."

The Ventriloquist was about to answer when he heard a sound.

BEEP BEEP! BEEP BEEP!

It took him a moment to realize his phone was ringing.

Wesker looked at the Penguin and then reached into his pocket. Quickly, he pulled out his phone.

"Hello?" he said.

"Dummy," said the voice on the other end.

"Mr. Scarface . . . ?" the Ventriloquist said, a look of genuine surprise on his face.

"Who else, Dummy?" said the voice. "I slipped away from the Penguin's goons."

"So you're okay? Where are you?" said the Ventriloquist. "I'm . . . I'm sort of in the middle of something here."

"I got other plans," said the voice on the phone. The Ventriloquist looked at the Penguin. Both of them appeared to be completely confused.

"What do you want me to do?" asked the Ventriloquist.

"We'll...go over this later," said the voice. "Get back."

"To the hideout?" said the Ventriloquist.

"Get back," the voice repeated.

"But —"

"Shut your mouth and get back!" Scarface growled.

CLICK.

The line went dead.

The Ventriloquist looked at his phone for a minute. Then he put it back in his pocket. He shrugged and said to the Penguin, "Um . . . never mind?"

Then the Ventriloquist waved his goons off and left.

The Penguin looked at his men. "What the heck was that?" he asked.

They all shrugged.

The Penguin sighed. "Whatever. Just go get the car."

The Penguin didn't speak for the entire drive back to his home. He simply had no idea what to say.

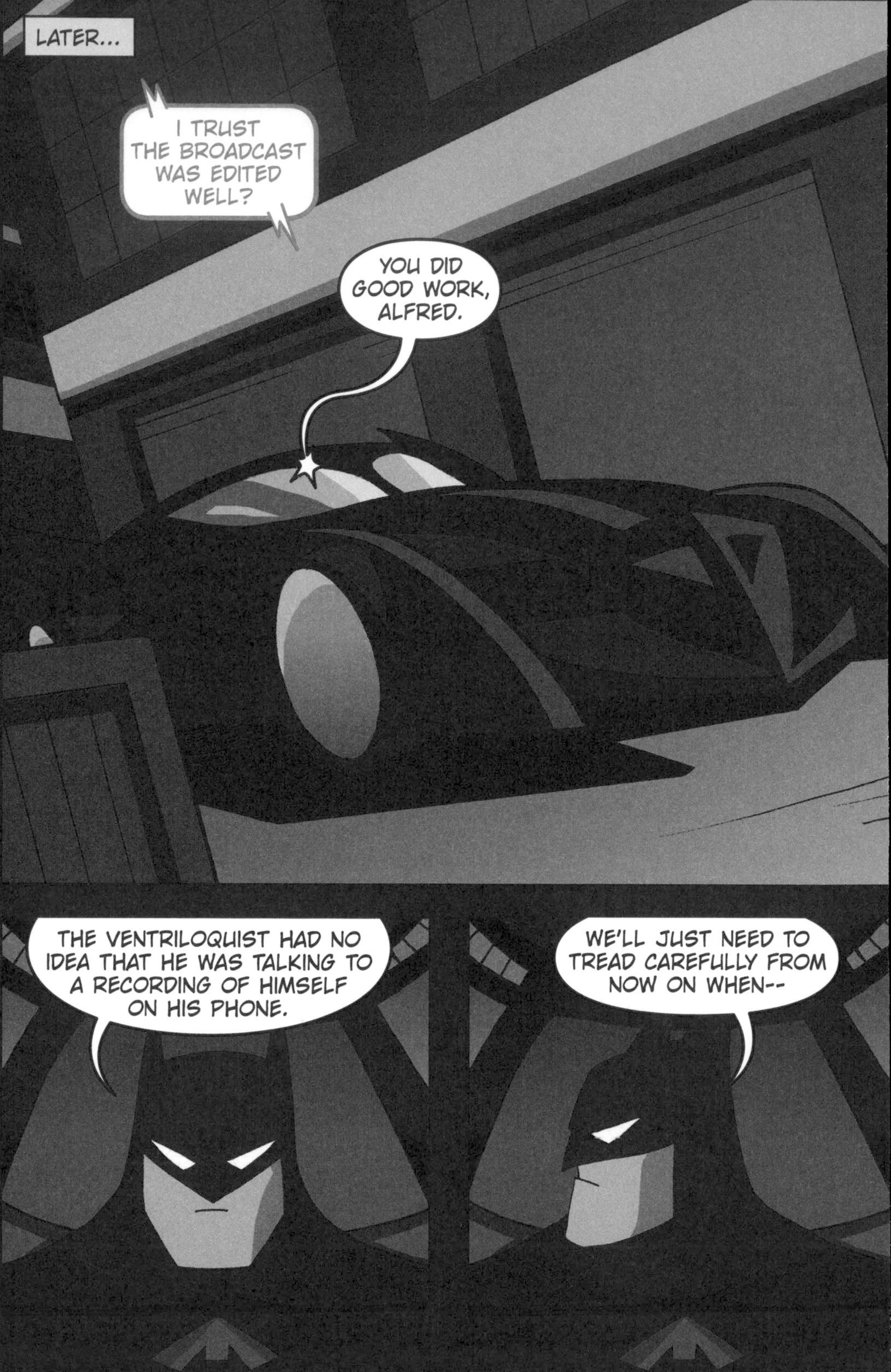
LATER...
I TRUST THE BROADCAST WAS EDITED WELL?
YOU DID GOOD WORK, ALFRED.
THE VENTRILOQUIST HAD NO IDEA THAT HE WAS TALKING TO A RECORDING OF HIMSELF ON HIS PHONE.
WE'LL JUST NEED TO TREAD CAREFULLY FROM NOW ON WHEN--

KNOCK! KNOCK!

Batman turned to face the passenger side of the Batmobile. There was a piece of paper taped to the outside of the window.

"Is everything all right, Master Bruce?" Alfred asked. "Is someone else there?"

Batman rolled down his window and grabbed the piece of paper. "Nice working with you, officer," he read the note aloud.

"Sir?" Alfred asked.

CLICK!

Batman pressed a button that raised the Batmobile's canopy. He glanced up at the tall building stretching above the alley. Disappearing over the ledge of the building was Catwoman's shadowy form.

"Sir," Alfred said, "I must insist you respond. I'm getting concerned."

"Never mind, Alfred," Batman said, smiling. "It's nothing to worry about."

* * *

THUMP!

Catwoman landed gracefully on the fire escape leading to her apartment. Then she stood up and stretched. She had successfully returned Scarface to the Ventriloquist's home without incident, just as Batman had asked her to do.

She sighed. It had been a long couple of days, and she was excited to curl up on her bed in front of an old movie. She needed to get her mind off the fact that the Penguin would most certainly not be paying her for her efforts now.

But was smiling ear to ear, comforted by the knowledge that she still had her trophy from the other night's heist.

She opened the window.

CRRREAAAAK!

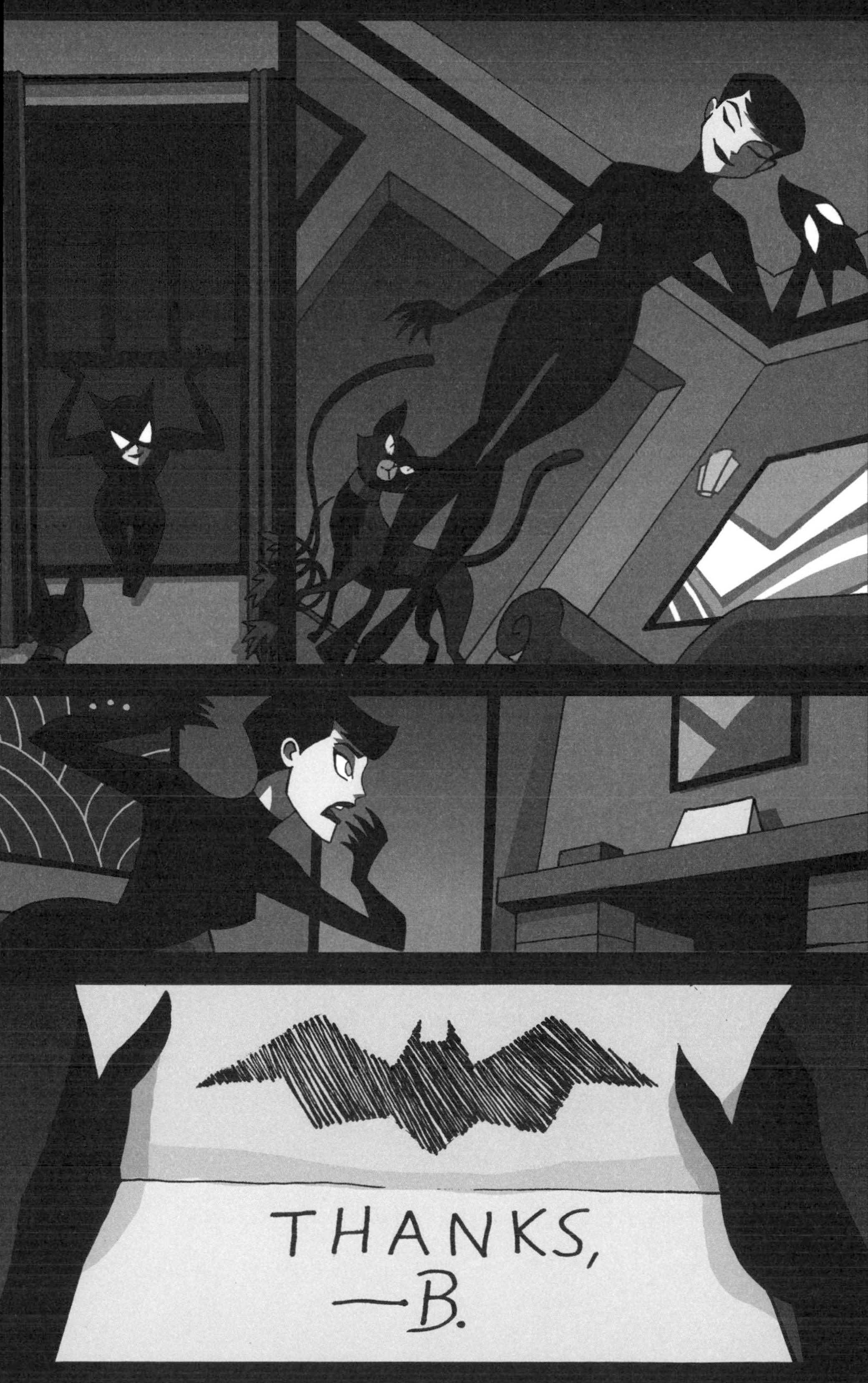
THANKS,
—B.

Selina rubbed her eyes with her fingers. "You're welcome, Batman," she said through clenched teeth.

CATWOMAN

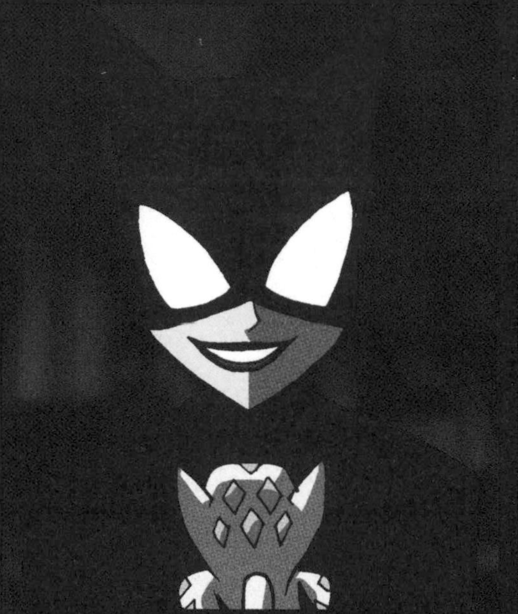

REAL NAME:
Selina Kyle

OCCUPATION:
Professional Thief

BASE:
Gotham City

HEIGHT:
5 feet 7 inches

WEIGHT:
125 pounds

EYES:
Blue

HAIR:
Black

Like Bruce Wayne, Selina Kyle was orphaned at a young age. But unlike Bruce, Selina had no caretakers or family fortune to support her. Growing up alone on the mean streets of Gotham City, Selina resorted to petty crime in order to survive. She soon became one of the city's most talented criminals. As Catwoman, Selina prowls the streets of Gotham, preying on the wealthy while guarding Gotham's fellow castaways.

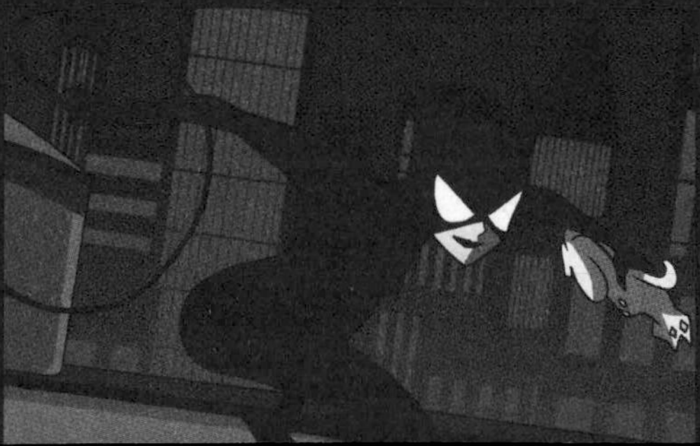

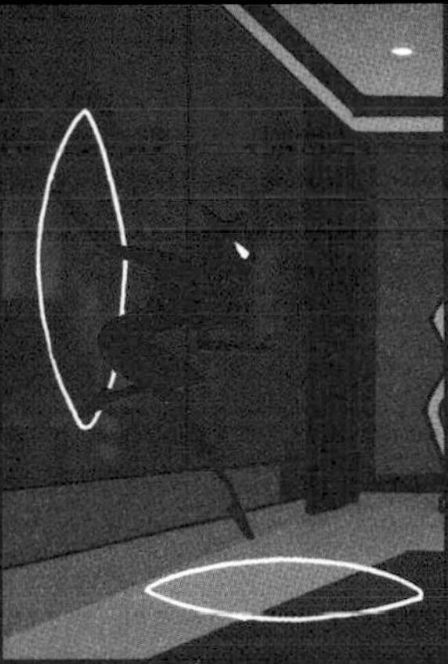

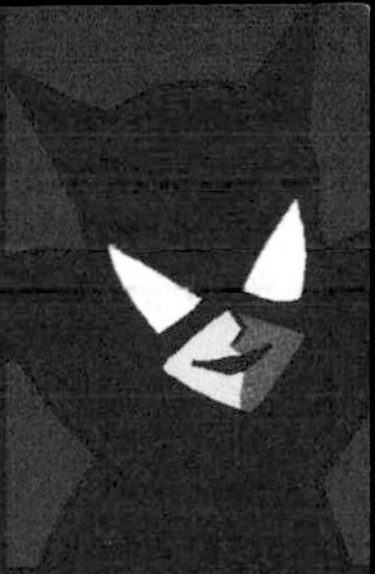

- Selina's love of felines inspired her cat-related nickname. In fact, much of her stolen loot has been donated to cat-saving charities.
- The athletic Selina prefers to use her feline agility to evade her foes, but she won't hesitate to use her retractable claws if she's cornered.
- Catwoman may be a hardened criminal, but she does have a soft spot for Gotham City's orphans. Proceeds from her crimes often go to local orphanages and foster homes.

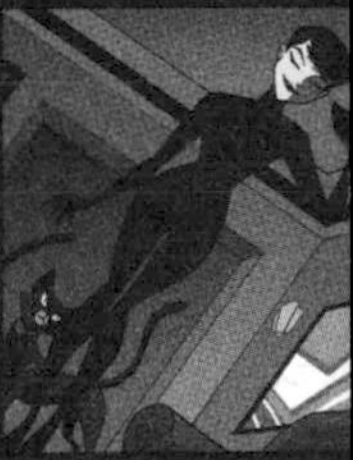

- Selina has been an ally to Batman several times. However, their alliances never last, since Selina is disinterested in ending her thieving ways.

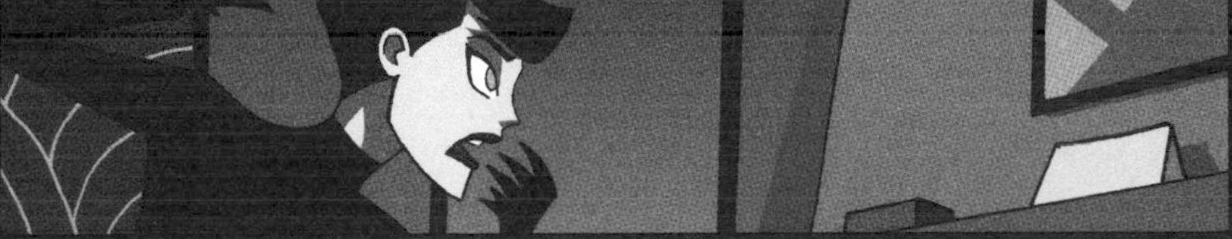

BIOGRAPHIES

MATT MANNING is the author of many books and comics, from the massive Andrews McMeel hardcover *The Batman Files* to single issues of comic books featuring Looney Tunes. He recently penned a mini-series for DC Comics, and is developing another new and original series. He lives in Mystic, Connecticut with his wife, Dorothy, and his daughter, Lillian.

LUCIANO VECCHIO was born in 1982 and currently lives in Buenos Aires, Argentina. With experience in illustration, animation, and comics, his works have been published in the US, Spain, the UK, France, and Argentina. His credits include Ben 10 (DC Comics), Cruel Thing (Norma), Unseen Tribe (Zuda Comics), and Sentinels (Drumfish Productions).

SKETCHES

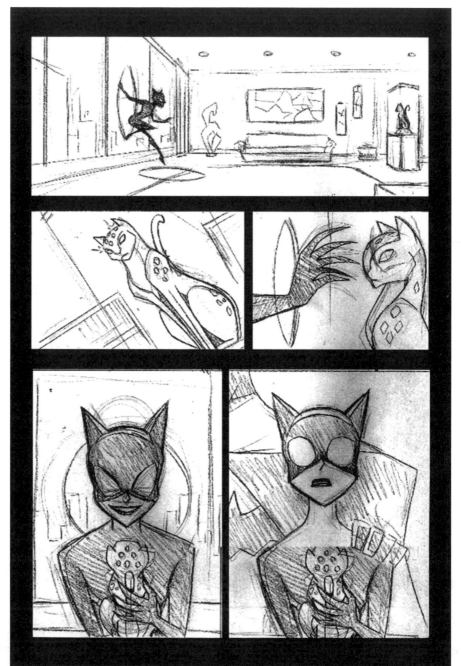

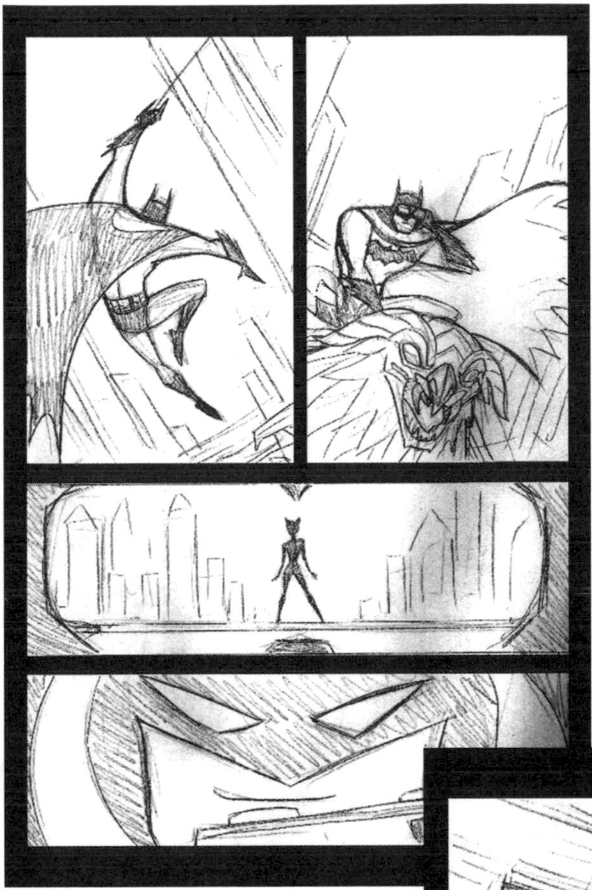
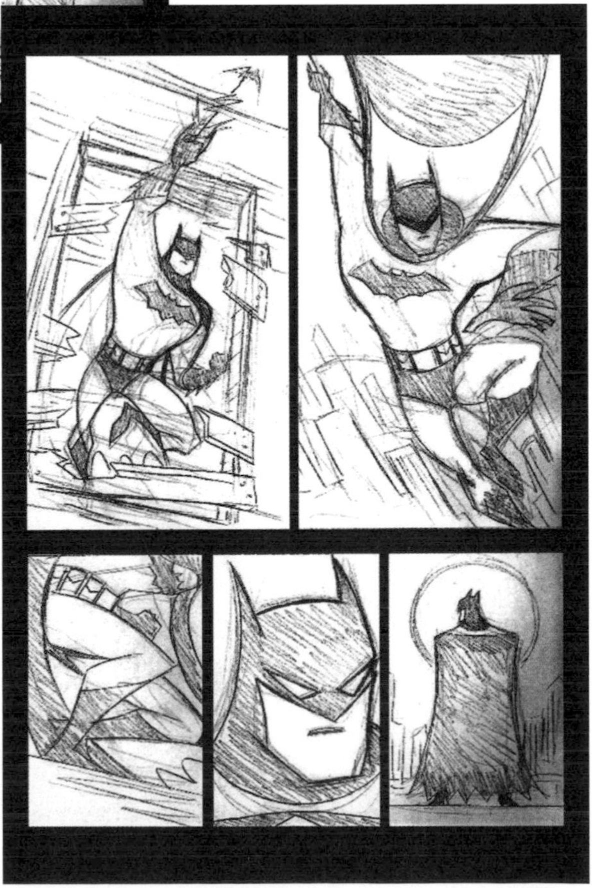

FINAL ART

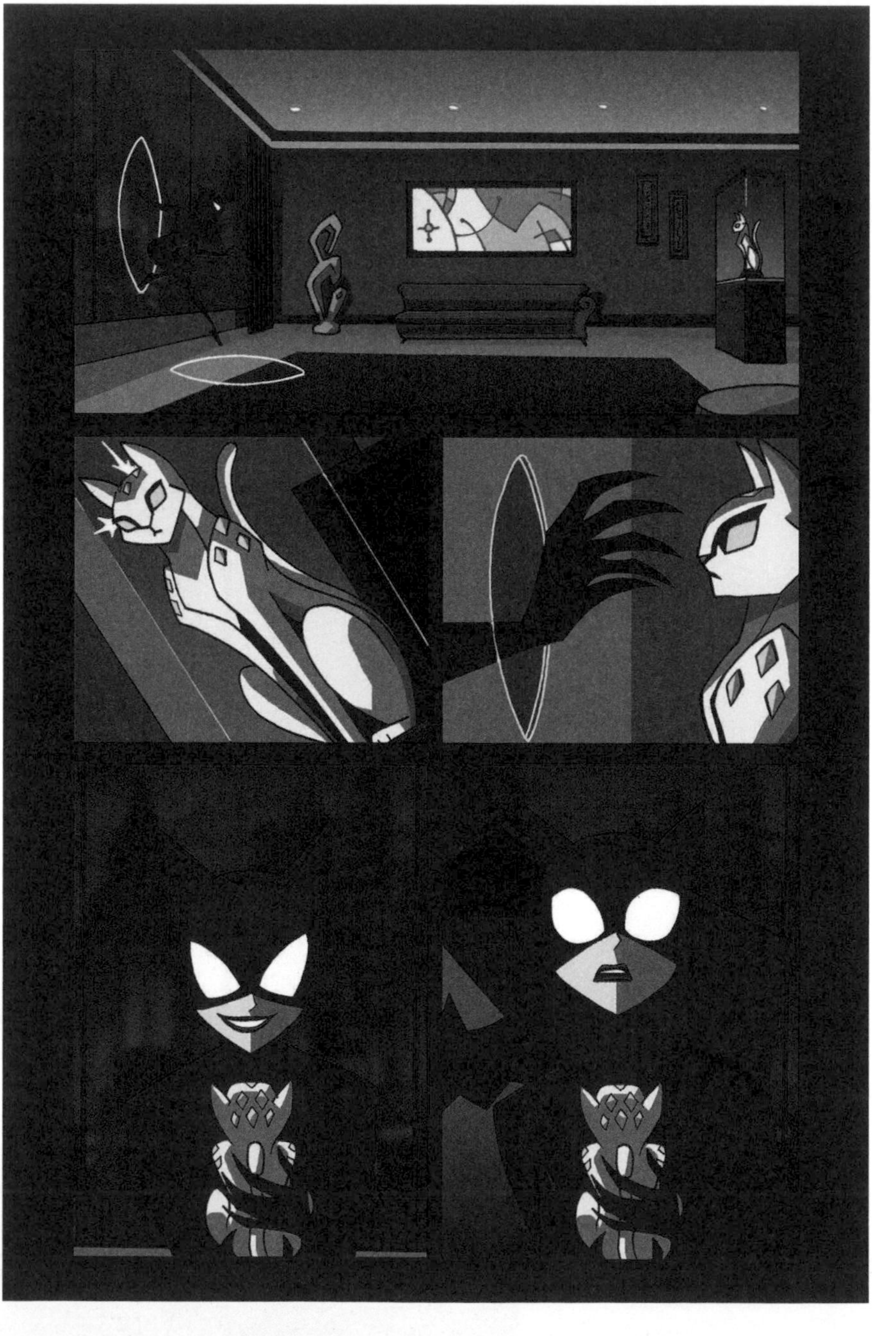

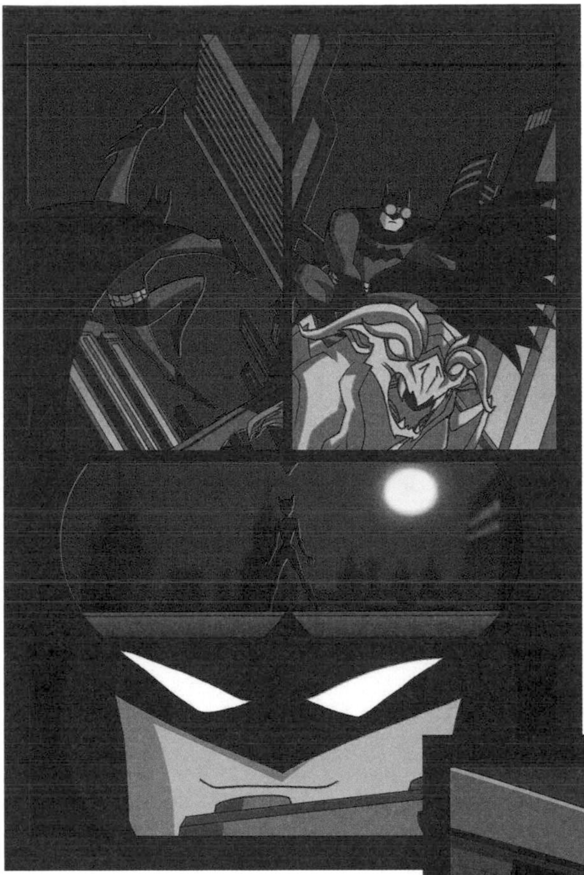
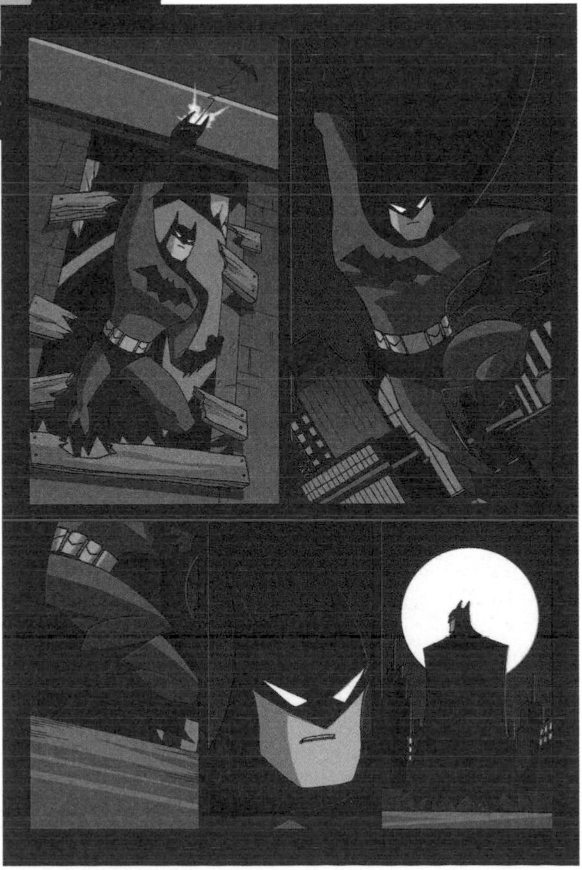

COMICS TERMS

caption (KAP-shuhn)—words that appear in a box. Captions are often used to set the scene.

gutter (GUHT-er)—the space between panels or pages

motion lines (MOH-shuhn LINES)—illustrator-created marks that help show motion in art

panel (PAN-uhl)—a single drawing that has borders around it. Each panel is a separate scene on a spread.

SFX (ESS-EFF-EKS)—short for sound effects. Sound effects are words used to show sounds that occur in the art of a comic.

splash (SPLASH)—a large illustration that often covers a full page (or more)

spread (SPRED)—two side-by-side pages in a comic book

word balloon (WURD BUH-loon)—a speech indicator that includes a character's dialogue or thoughts. A word balloon's tail leads to the speaking character's mouth.

GLOSSARY

ambitious (am-BISH-uhss)—having a desire to be successful, powerful, or famous

Batarang (BAT-uh-rang)—a boomerang-like projectile Batman often uses in battle

braced (BRAYSSD)—prepared for something difficult or unpleasant

dummy (DUHM-ee)—a doll shaped like a person that is often used by a ventriloquist

dysfunctional (dis-FUNK-shun-uhl)—troubled

elusive (i-LOO-siv)—hard to understand, define, or catch hold of

obsessed (uhb-SESSD)—overly attached to something or someone

penthouse (PENT-house)—a fancy apartment at the very top of a building

rappel (ruh-PELL)—to move down a steep surface by pushing your feet against it and sliding down a rope

threat (THRET)—potential danger or harm

VISUAL QUESTIONS

1. Batman and Catwoman play cat and mouse over the streets of Gotham City. What are some clever tricks Batman and Catwoman used?

2. Why did Catwoman's expression change in the gutter, or the space between these two panels below? How do you think she feels in each shot?

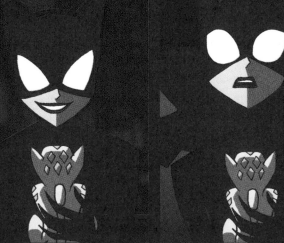

3. Why did the Ventriloquist snap his fingers when he did? What is the "reveal" in the second panel?

4. Describe Selina and Batman's friendship. Why do they make a good team? Why do they make a bad team?